"I just can't stop worrying about Robbie, not for a single moment," Ali said

Logan walked over and sat down on the edge of the bed. "He'll be home in just a little while—in time for Christmas."

"And will he be the same happy boy?" she murmured.

"He'll be fine." He *had* to be. Ali didn't deserve anything less than a perfectly happy ending. She leaned against him, all softness and warmth. How could he want her so much when the timing was impossible?

"Logan?" she whispered.

"Uh-huh?"

"Would you do something for me?"

"Sure. What?"

"Would you stay here with me for a while?"

"I'll just sit here with you," he whispered. He switched off the bedside lamp and merely held her, willing away his aching desire....

Dear Reader,

At Harlequin Intrigue, we all agree—nothing is better on a cold winter night than cozying up with a good romantic mystery. So we've asked some of our favorite authors—and yours—to entertain us with some special stories this month, which are set around the holidays.

We hope you'll grab some cider and cuddle up with *I'll Be Home for Christmas* by Dawn Stewardson—a Christmas mystery that we know will warm your heart!

Sincerely,

Debra Matteucci
Senior Editor & Editorial Coordinator
Harlequin Books
300 East 42nd Street
New York, NY 10017

Dawn Stewardson
I'll Be Home for Christmas

Harlequin Books

TORONTO • NEW YORK • LONDON
AMSTERDAM • PARIS • SYDNEY • HAMBURG
STOCKHOLM • ATHENS • TOKYO • MILAN
MADRID • WARSAW • BUDAPEST • AUCKLAND

To D'Arcy Lynn Stewardson and Bob Hacking,
who helped play with the plot.

And to John, always.

ISBN 0-373-22302-1

I'LL BE HOME FOR CHRISTMAS

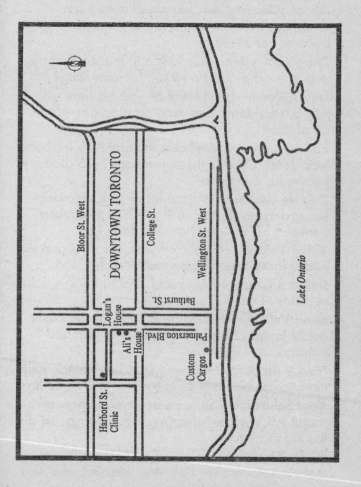

CAST OF CHARACTERS

Ali Weyden—When her six-year-old son vanished, every mother's worst nightmare became her reality.

Robbie Weyden—His kidnapper said the boy was safe. The question was, for how long?

Logan Reed—He'd been biding his time with Ali, but suddenly time was running out—for all of them.

Bob Weyden—Everybody thought Ali's husband was dead. Or was there someone who'd always known he was alive?

Celeste Weyden—Ali's mother-in-law loved her grandson. But what if she had to choose between his life and her own son's?

Vinny Velarde—Bob Weyden's business partner had a lot to lose if Bob wasn't really dead.

Deloras Gayle—How much did Vinny's secretary know?

Mimi Velarde—Vinny's wife was mysteriously out of town. Could she be the one who had Robbie?

Nancy McGuire—Ali was sure her friend would never cross her. Not even for two million dollars.

Kent Schiraldi—Nancy's boyfriend knew all about Ali Weyden's money. Mysteriously, so did the kidnapper.

Nicky Sinclair and *Chico Gonzalez*—These mobsters were after Bob Weyden. But who else was in danger from them?

Chapter One

He hung up and allowed himself a relieved smile. Finding out what he'd needed to know had been almost too easy. And the situation would be almost too perfect.

It was enough to start him worrying that he was missing something crucial.

Going over the plan in detail once more, he decided he wasn't. He had plenty of time to scope the layout, find the room, figure out the best place to make the snatch. And no doubt every little rug rat in the neighborhood would be there, making for total pandemonium. With a whole roomful of excited kids, nobody was going to miss one small boy in the time it would take to grab him.

Glancing at what he'd jotted down, he checked it a final time, making certain there was nothing more he needed to know.

Sunday, December 18. Harbord Street Children's Clinic. Activities room. Three till six.

That definitely took care of it, nothing he'd forget, so he lit a match to one corner of the paper, then dropped it into the empty trash can and watched it burn.

On the radio, the announcer's baritone rolled over the final strains of "Jingle Bell Rock."

"We're going to take a short newsbreak, folks, see what's happening on the snowy streets of Toronto. It's colder than a witch's kiss out there, but it's hot, hot, hot here on CTOR, big-city radio. And when we come back we'll have a song for everyone leaving the big T.O. to spend the holidays with family. We've got the King himself, cued to sing 'I'll Be Home for Christmas.'"

He couldn't contain a second smile—even more relaxed, now that he felt certain things would go his way. I'll be home for Christmas. He liked the sound of that. He'd remember to have the boy say it when the time came.

LOGAN REED PULLED into his narrow driveway, the Cherokee's tires crunching the inch of new snow that had fallen over the past couple of hours.

That triggered a thought, so he wrote a quick reminder. *Killer's car leaves clear tread marks in fresh snow.* He stuck it into the folder that held his notes on how to lift a strangler's fingerprints from a victim's throat, then climbed out of the Jeep and into the subzero afternoon.

The wind wrapped its icy fingers around his neck, so he zipped his bomber jacket the rest of the way up, reminding himself he'd soon be trading Canadian winter for California sunshine—or L.A. smog, if he wanted to be cynical about it. In some ways the move couldn't come soon enough. In others . . . well, there were a lot of things he'd miss about Toronto.

His breath forming tiny clouds, he strode along the slippery sidewalk, past the two houses that separated his from Ali Weyden's, thinking that the cold wasn't one of them. This neighborhood was, though. As close as it was to downtown, its streets were quiet, safe and peaceful—emanating a sense of stability that he doubted existed anywhere in L.A.

Most of the trees here had put down their roots a century ago, and the big brick houses exuded the charm of faded grandeur. Especially those on Palmerston. Take away the parked cars, and the entire street would look much as it had decades ago, right down to its original streetlamps—ornate wrought-iron standards, each topped by a large white globe.

He climbed the steps to Ali's front porch and turned the knob that rang the old-fashioned doorbell, wishing he didn't have to tell her he'd be abandoning her to the perilous world of paid baby-sitters. The shared child-care arrangement they'd fallen into had beaten that all to hell, and while he'd always had his parents to rely on in emergencies, Ali didn't have that sort of safety net. Her mother was dead, her only sister lived in Vancouver, and she'd never mentioned her father. So even if he was alive they couldn't be close.

He was reaching for the bell again when Ali appeared at the door. If he hadn't known better, he'd have taken her for eighteen rather than twenty-eight. Since she'd gone back to university in the fall as a "mature student," she'd been looking less mature by the week.

Today she had on jeans that were so baggy they probably contained twice as much denim as his, an equally baggy black sweater, and pink bunny slippers that were bigger than live snowshoe hares.

"You murder the short couple while I was gone?" he asked, looking past her into the empty hall. Nine times out of ten, it was the boys who answered the door. "Plan on pleading justifiable homicide?"

She smiled and shook her head. "I think writing crime fiction has warped your brain. But come on in and I'll make coffee. The 'short couple' is wreaking havoc in the basement, and I'm under orders not to disturb them. Not even for you."

When he stepped in out of the cold, the welcoming warmth smelled of Christmas. The aroma of fresh baking was wafting from the kitchen and mingling with the scent of pine from the tree he'd helped her wrestle into the house.

Glancing into the living room, he noted that the presents beneath it had been multiplying at a great rate. Then he turned his attention to tugging off his snowy cowboy boots—glad to see there were no holes in his socks.

"To quote your son," Ali was saying, "they can't be interrupted because they're making something 'top secret.'"

"Like a bomb?"

"Don't worry, I always keep that possibility in mind, but I think today it's just our Christmas presents. They're using mason jars, uncooked macaroni, finger paints, glue and gold glitter, so be prepared for the worst."

When Logan grimaced she rewarded him with another smile. She had an inordinately nice smile. In fact, most everything she had was inordinately nice. That had started him wondering, way back, whether she thought of him *only* as Cody's father.

Tossing his jacket onto the coat tree, he followed her past the stairs and along to the kitchen. Months ago, he'd decided that one day he was going to check out just exactly how she *did* think of him. But she tended to maneuver around personal questions, and he wasn't sure exactly how long she'd been widowed before she'd moved onto Palmerston. That had made him leery of pushing without any sign of encouragement from her. So he'd just been biding his time. And now it had suddenly become too late.

When they reached the big old kitchen he spotted the source of the baking smell—cookies cooling on the stove. It was the smells that gave her kitchen the homey feeling his lacked. He just never managed to get the kind of smells from his microwave that she produced with her oven.

"Chocolate chip?" he asked, doing his best not to drool.

"Half. Half are peanut butter. I had a sudden urge to bake. I suspect I'll be spending most of the Christmas break doing things I haven't had enough time for since September. Why don't you put some on a plate while I fix the coffee?"

"Hey, I wasn't hinting, you know."

"Sure you weren't." She flashed him a grin. "The boys don't need all of them, but watch the cookie sheet. It's still hot."

Logan dug a plate out of the cupboard and slid some cookies onto it, acquiring nothing worse than a first-degree burn to one finger. Then he sat down and watched Ali fiddling at the counter, thinking how he'd capture her appearance if she were a character in one of his novels.

He'd call her long hair either golden red or pale copper, he wasn't quite sure which. Her eyes were easier—big, brown and luminous. And her mouth... luscious was definitely the word that came to mind. Just as he'd ruled out thin for her figure, and decided on slender but shapely, she started over to the table with two mugs of coffee, asking him to get the milk.

He pushed back his chair and crossed to the fridge. There was a familiar-looking invitation stuck to its door with a pig magnet.

"You're going to this thing tomorrow?" he asked, gesturing to the invitation and glancing back at her.

"Uh-huh. One of my friends is a social worker at the clinic. Nancy McGuire? My age, shoulder-length brown hair, blue eyes?"

He shook his head to say he didn't know her. Most parents in the neighborhood took their children to the clinic, because it had a family feel. But he and Cody had only met the doctors and nurses.

"Well, anyway, it was Nancy who sent the invitation," Ali told him as he grabbed the milk carton and headed back to the table. "She said Robbie would love it."

"He will. Cody had so much candy at it last year he was sick the next day. But would you do me a favor since you're going? Take Cody, too?"

"Sure, no problem. You've got something else on?"

"Not something *else,* but I have to get there early. As of this morning I'm their Santa. The original volunteer broke his arm—slipped on some ice."

"Oh? I'm surprised Cody wasn't bubbling over with the news. Having a father stand in for the real Mr. Claus has to be big stuff."

"That's exactly why I'm keeping it a secret until tomorrow. He'd want the whole world to know, so I'd have half the kids in the neighborhood climbing on my knee and saying, 'Hi, Mr. Reed.'"

Ali eyed him for a moment, trying to picture him as old Saint Nick. It wasn't easy, not even when she imagined him in a red suit rather than jeans and that creamy fisherman sweater. Logan Reed was all lean muscles and chiseled features—definitely appealing on real men, but hardly choice Santa Claus material.

"What?" he demanded. "You don't think I'll be any good?"

His injured expression was so blatantly phony that she laughed. "Well, let's see. You're thirty-three, right? And Santa's supposed to be what...eighty-something? Your hair is brown, not white, and it's neither curly nor as long as his, and—"

"Wait a minute. I've got blue eyes. *That's* a match."

"All right, I'll give you the eyes." She could hardly not. They were the bluest eyes she'd ever seen. "But you're clean-shaven and Santa's got whiskers down to his belt. And you can't weigh more than...a hundred and eighty?"

"One-seventy-five."

"Even worse," she teased. "But I guess, aside from those few *minor* details..."

"So, you haven't heard of padding? And false beards and wigs? Hey, give me a couple of pillows and I'll be terrific. By tomorrow, I'm going to have the best 'ho-ho-ho' you've ever heard. Just wait and see."

That made her laugh again. Logan was easy to be around. So much so, that when they'd first met she'd been surprised to learn he was unattached. She assumed marriage had left him feeling much the way it had her—once bitten, twice shy. Still, she knew he'd been divorced for years, and it seemed strange that *some* woman hadn't managed to wangle her way into his life. He had that rugged kind of attractiveness a lot of women went for. In fact, if she had any interest in men, even *she* might...

But she had *no* interest in men. At the moment, the only important things were getting her life on track and ensuring that Robbie was happy.

"Ali?"

She glanced across the table and Logan caught her gaze in the blue depth of his. She felt the little sexual tug that completely belied her *total* disinterest in men—in this particular one, at least. And it was a tug she'd been feeling more and more often recently when she was near him.

"There's something I have to tell you," Logan said. "I heard from L.A. yesterday. My film agent called and she pulled it off. I get to collaborate on the script."

"Oh, Logan, that's wonderful. You must be thrilled."

"I am. Connie worked a miracle. Hollywood *hates* to let an author adapt his novel for the screen, unless he's someone who's already done it a dozen times."

"But you were dying for the chance, weren't you."

He nodded. "Doing the screenplay gives you a shot at keeping the story's integrity intact. Otherwise, you've got absolutely no control over it."

"This way you will, though. Oh, I'm really, really happy for you. What a great Christmas present."

"There's one catch," he said after a moment. "It means Cody and I have to move to L.A. At least until the film's in the can."

That little news flash took her completely by surprise, and she suddenly wasn't quite as happy for him. It was totally selfish, of course, but she'd miss having him around...miss it more than a little. And Robbie would miss Cody. The boys had been inseparable since the day they'd met.

"I feel badly about leaving you in the lurch for a sitter," Logan said.

"Don't. I'll work something out. But how long until the film's 'in the can'?"

He shrugged. "It depends. They want me there by the end of January, and it'll take three or four months to work on the script. Then however long the shooting takes. But they've optioned two of my other books, so...well, the move *could* turn out to be permanent."

"Oh."

He caught her gaze again. This time she glanced away, trying to ignore the ridiculous feeling that he was abandoning her. They were friends, nothing more.

That's the way she'd wanted it. And friends came and went in life.

"Robbie will be devastated when he hears," she said.

"Well, don't say anything yet. I'm not going to tell Cody we're going until after Christmas. And I'll be keeping the house for the time being. See what the situation looks like in a few months, then decide whether or not to sell it."

She nodded. He was already considering selling. The more he told her, the more it sounded as if *permanent* was a foregone conclusion.

Strange how things worked out. Or *didn't* work out, as the case might be. She'd been living two doors away from Logan for almost a year, yet it had only been in the past few months that he'd been making her feel... She couldn't quite describe it, but lately, every time she looked at his broad shoulders, or he smiled at her with his sensual smile, she felt . . . a hot little rush of excitement. That was as close as she could come to describing the feeling. And the way it had been getting stronger and stronger had started her thinking that maybe...

But her timing with men was apparently no better than her taste in them had ever been.

"Do you like the idea of living in L.A.?" she finally asked.

"I haven't had much time to think about it. I always figured one of the benefits to writing was that you can do it anywhere. But according to Connie, *no one* writes for Hollywood without living in L.A. You have to be on hand for a hundred different reasons. So

I can write novels living there, but I can't do scripts living here." He raised his hands, palms up, saying he had no choice.

"The boys will really miss each other...whether it turns out to be short-term or long."

As if they'd picked up vibrations that said they were being talked about, Robbie and Cody thundered up from the basement. To Ali they sounded more like an invading army than two six-year-olds, and when they burst into the kitchen they replaced the calm with a whirlwind of chaos—chaos liberally smeared with finger paints and dusted with gold glitter.

"Cookies!" Robbie shouted, his dark eyes dancing. "You shoulda called us!"

"Dad!" Cody yelled. "Dad, I made you the neatest thing, but you can't see it. Not till Christmas Day."

"Me, too, Mom," Robbie assured her. "Can we have pop with the cookies?"

"Milk," she said firmly, nodding at the carton. "And pour *very* carefully."

"Milk?" Cody said, wrinkling his nose.

"Milk," Logan told him.

Wordlessly, the boys divided up the task—Cody getting the glasses, Robbie pouring. They managed it without mishap, then descended on the cookies like a couple of starving vultures attacking road kill.

Robbie grabbed one and stuffed the entire thing into his mouth at once—something Ali had told him at least ten thousand times he wasn't to do.

Then he grinned and gave her such an exaggerated "Mmmm" of appreciation that she laughed despite herself.

"Monsters," Logan muttered to her under his breath. "Neither of them is even slightly civilized, you know."

Ali looked at Robbie once more. He *could* be a monster at times, but he was the most important thing in her life. And whether he was uncivilized or not, she couldn't conceive of ever loving another human being as much as she loved her little monster.

CODY AND ROBBIE weren't exactly sitting beside Ali. More accurately, they were bouncing up and down on their chairs. But that seemed to be the norm in the room. There'd be a lot of parents going home from the party with migraines.

"I don't think I'm *ever* going to have kids of my own," Nancy said, looking past Ali at the boys. Her words were almost lost in the low-level roar that filled the activities room.

"Sounds like a good game plan to me," Kent muttered from beside her. "If you'd warned me how crazy these no-necks would get, you'd never have lured me away from the Cowboys-Redskins game."

"Kids are only *really* scary when they outnumber the adults like this," Ali teased. "It's their primitive pack mentality that's so frightening." She glanced past Nancy to Kent as she finished speaking, trying to decide if he'd been serious about not wanting children.

She knew Nancy had been joking, but she'd had years of exposure to Nancy's sardonic sense of humor. They went way back, had met during Ali's first time around at university.

Kent Schiraldi, though, she couldn't read with any consistency, despite having known him for a couple of years. She'd met him, socially, just after he'd started going with Nancy. And recently, he'd helped her out professionally, by investing the proceeds from Bob's insurance policy.

He was a big, good-looking guy who'd played a lot of sports in college and kept in shape. And he certainly wasn't short in the brains department. Beyond that, though, Ali just didn't feel as if she really knew him.

"Ms. Weyden?" Cody said, tugging on her sleeve. "Are you *sure* me an' Robbie have to go last?"

She told herself to be patient, even though he'd already asked the question about fifty times.

"That's the way your dad wants it," she explained again. "I think," she whispered, turning back to Nancy, "Logan's afraid Cody will try to pull off his beard to let all the kids see it's his father."

"But, Mom," Robbie said, "there aren't many presents left. What if he runs out before it's our turn?"

"He won't run out, love," Nancy assured him.

"Did you count them? And count all the kids?"

"Somebody did."

"But what if it's only *girl* presents left?" he demanded. "Cody, what if we got *Barbies?*" He gave an exaggerated shudder that sent Cody into a fit of giggles.

"There'll be boy presents left," Nancy promised.

"*We* should count," Robbie suggested, poking Cody. "Count the presents beside your dad and count the kids in line."

As the junior statisticians went to work, Ali absently gazed toward the front of the room, where Logan had a smiling little girl on his knee.

Santa's throne had been set up in front of a series of divider panels covered in red felt, and it was surrounded by a forest of decorated pine trees. The children were lined up to Santa's left and made their way along a winding path to his throne. Then, after their minute or two of glory with him, they followed another path to the far side to rejoin their waiting parents. Whoever had decorated had done an outstanding job.

"Hey," Nancy whispered to get Ali's attention. "How come you've never told me about Cody's father?"

"I *have*," she whispered back.

"No, you haven't. I'd remember."

"I'm *positive* I have. The neighbor who's always looking after Robbie?"

"*That's* the neighbor?"

Ali nodded.

"Well, you sure left out all the good stuff, then. Someone introduced us before he changed into the Santa suit, and he's an absolute hunk."

"I guess he's not bad."

"Not bad? I think you'd better get your eyes checked. And when you said a divorced neighbor, I assumed you were talking about a housewife. But this guy... what's the story?"

"There's *no* story—except that being a novelist means he works at home, so we trade baby-sitting a lot. At least we *have* been, but he's moving out of town soon. Don't say anything about that in front of the boys, though," she added in a whisper.

"Mom?" Robbie said. "Mom, there's no other kids. Just us. And the line's almost gone. So me and Cody gotta get in it now."

"Cody and I," she automatically corrected him.

"Okay!" Cody shrieked, scrambling off his chair. "Let's go, Robbie!"

Ali followed them into the aisle and stood absently watching Logan while they waited. He'd been right about making a terrific Santa. The kids loved him. She began thinking, once again, how much she was going to miss having him and Cody around, then made a conscious effort to stop.

Thinking she'd miss them wouldn't change the facts. And odds were, once they went to L.A. they'd be gone for good. Some gorgeous starlet would grab Logan and never let him go, because Nancy was right. He was an absolute hunk.

Maybe she shouldn't have done such a good job of ignoring that for so many months. If she hadn't been quite so intent on keeping men at the bottom of her priorities list, she and Logan might have . . .

Absently, she pushed her hair back from her face, knowing it was pointless to speculate. She'd always had poor judgment when it came to men. Still, she'd always imagined what things would be like with the *right* man.

If Logan Reed was Mr. Right, though, she'd waited too long to find out. Besides, she'd never been lucky in love, so what had started her thinking fate might have been ready to make an exception? The adult-size elf at the head of the line began speaking to Robbie, drawing Ali's attention back to the present.

"It'll be your turn in just another few seconds," the woman was saying. "I'll tell you when to go, but don't run, okay?"

"Okay." He grinned at Ali, and she knelt down between him and Cody.

"I'm going over to the other side, now, so I can meet you both when you're finished."

"And after me and Robbie, my dad's done, right?" Cody said. "And I go home with *him,* not you and Robbie, right?"

"As far as I know, that's the plan, Cody." She gave them each a quick hug, started off, then stopped halfway across the back of the room when a man called, "Ali?" Turning, she was surprised to see it was Kent Schiraldi. She hadn't noticed him leaving his seat.

"Talk to you for a minute?" he asked.

"Sure." She looked around for Nancy, but didn't see her.

"Nance went to her office," he explained. "And I thought it might be a good time to ask you about something."

A quick glance told her Robbie was safely ensconced on Santa's knee, and she looked back at Kent.

"I realize you're Nance's friend, not mine," he said quietly, "but I don't know who else to ask."

"All right. Ask away."

"Ali...I think Nance is involved with someone else. Is she?"

He stared directly into her eyes, obviously hoping to see the truth there, regardless of her words.

"Is she?" he repeated.

Ali shook her head. "No. I mean, if she is, she hasn't said anything about it to me."

"And she would have, wouldn't she?"

"I . . . probably. But what makes you think she is?"

"Somebody's phoned a couple of times when I've been at her place. And it's like she didn't want to talk to him in front of me."

"You're sure it was a *him?*"

"I got that feeling. And, lately, I've just had the sense that something's going on she's keeping from me."

"Have you asked her about it?"

"Yeah, and she denies there's anything. But she's a little *too* defensive, you know? Just now, I asked her while you were in line with the boys, and she said that if I didn't believe her, why didn't I ask you. Then she just got up and said she had to go to her office. So I thought, why *not* ask you?"

"Well, she really hasn't said a word. But..."

Ali paused, glancing up to the front of the room again. It was Cody who was with Santa now. "Look, Kent, I've got to go get Robbie, but is there anything I can do to help? Do you want me to talk to her?"

He shrugged. "If you could convince her to tell me what's going on . . . not knowing is driving me nuts."

"All right, then why don't we go out for pizza after the party? And I'll make a point to get her alone and see what I can do."

"That would be great."

"There's probably nothing wrong, though."

"Yeah. Maybe not."

Ali gave him a reassuring smile, then turned and started toward the front of the room.

Even though Logan still had Cody on his knee, a few people were already getting ready to leave—shrugging into their coats and blocking her way. Likely some of the same people, she thought with annoyance, who left Blue Jays games halfway through the eighth inning, no matter who was ahead.

When she finally made it to the front, Cody was tightly clutching a present while Logan was waving to the crowd. He gave a loud "Ho-ho-ho," then called, "Goodbye until Christmas Eve, boys and girls."

She couldn't see Robbie anywhere, and behind her everyone in the room seemed to be standing up. She swore to herself. Now she'd have to find a three-foot-ten-inch boy among a bunch of six-foot-tall adults. She started through the crowd, her gaze catching on at least a dozen brown-haired little boys who weren't her son.

When she reached the back wall she spotted the men's room and stopped, a little surge of hope rushing through her. She had a rule about Robbie not going into strange washrooms like this by himself, but maybe he'd been desperate.

"Excuse me?" she said, intercepting a man on his way in. "I'm looking for my son. Would you mind giving a shout and see if he's in there? His name's Robbie.''

"Sure." He stepped inside and called, "Robbie? Is there a Robbie here?"

A second later he stuck his head back out. "Sorry. Not in here."

She nodded her thanks, her mouth beginning to feel dry. Then it occurred to her that Robbie might have gone back to their seats.

Walking faster now, she headed in that direction. When she got to them, his jacket was still on his chair, between hers and Cody's. *He* was nowhere in sight, though. Her anxiety level had been rising rapidly, but she forced herself to look around slowly and carefully. He had to be *somewhere* in the room.

The crowd was thinning, so she should be able to spot him . . . but she couldn't. She didn't see a single child who wasn't with an adult.

She did see Logan and Cody, though, heading toward her, Logan still in his Santa outfit. When they reached her, she took a deep breath and tried not to sound as if she was nearing panic state. "Logan, I don't know where Robbie is."

"Maybe he's still with the man," Cody said.

Her heart stopped beating.

Logan crouched down and rested his hands on Cody's shoulders. "What man, son?" he asked quietly.

"The man he went with."

Chapter Two

Ali began praying she'd wake up and find this was a nightmare, because she couldn't really be here and this couldn't really be happening.

But she knew it *wasn't* a nightmare. Someone, some man, had stolen her son. Every mother's worst fear had become her reality.

"What man, Cody?" Logan asked quietly.

Cody shrugged. "I don't know. I didn't see him."

"But you just said Robbie went with him, so you must have seen him."

"No. I just saw a piece of him. Just his arm and hand."

"But how could you see Robbie going with him if you couldn't see more than that?"

"Well...I could just kinda see."

Ali had an almost overwhelming urge to grab Cody and try shaking the details out of him. But she knew that would only make him cry, so she just wrapped her arms around herself to keep from trembling. Her skin felt burning hot and clammy at the same time, and her stomach had begun churning.

"What do you mean, you could *kinda* see?" Logan was asking.

"I mean I just saw for a minute. When I was getting on your knee."

"Cody, tell me *exactly* what you saw."

"Dad, is Robbie okay?"

"I'm sure he's fine, son. Just tell me exactly what you saw."

"Well . . . Robbie was walking. Then he stopped. I guess the man said something to him. Then the man put his hand on his shoulder. That's how come I saw his arm."

"But that's *all* you saw?"

"Uh-huh. Just his arm."

"And did he have on a sweater? Or a jacket? What?"

"A coat. A coat kinda like Grandpa's. And gloves like Grandpa's, too."

"And where was he? When he stopped Robbie?"

Cody pointed in the direction of the throne. "By those red things. Robbie was on this side, but the man was on the other side. That's how come I just saw his arm. He was kinda reaching between two of those red things."

"Logan?" Ali whispered, her throat so tight she could barely manage his name. She glanced at the red dividers.

"It's going to be all right, Ali." He hoisted Cody to his shoulder, then firmly grabbed her hand. "We'll just go have a look back there."

As they hurried forward, she realized that all the glittering Christmas trees practically blocked the lower halves of the divider panels from view. So if a man had been crouched behind one of them, if he'd stopped Robbie as he'd been walking away from his visit with Santa, would anyone have even noticed?

She bit her lip, trying to hold back the tears burning her eyes, and silently repeated Logan's words. It was going to be all right.

It *had* to be all right.

As they neared the throne, Logan lowered Cody to the floor. Then he shoved one of the panels aside so they could step behind them. A few feet along the back wall was a fire exit. A stick cracked the door open to the evening darkness.

Her heart hammering in horror, Ali stood staring at the exit. Beside her, Logan ripped off his beard and Santa hat and tossed them onto a nearby chair, saying, "Ali, listen to me."

It sounded as if he was speaking through dense fog.

"Listen to me," he repeated. He took her by the shoulders and turned her to face him. "You've got to hang tough. We can't be *certain* someone took Robbie. Maybe it just *looked* that way. Maybe he's just in another part of the building. Or he might have wandered outside on his own."

She closed her eyes in silent anguish. Robbie wouldn't have wandered *anywhere* without telling her. But why would he have gone off with a stranger without making a fuss? He knew never to do that.

"Dad?" Cody said, his voice quavering. "Dad, what if Robbie *is* gone? What if the man disappeared him?"

"Don't worry about *what if* just now, son. I'm pretty sure Robbie's going to be okay. But are *you* going to be all right, Ali?"

She nodded, desperately trying to fight the woozy sensation that was making her feel more ill by the second.

"Fine," Logan said, giving her shoulders a hard squeeze. "We've got to start searching. Can you cope with that?"

Too numb to speak, she merely nodded again. If there was a chance they could find her son, she'd cope with whatever she had to.

"Good." He glanced into the main area of the room, then back at her. "What was that guy's name? The one who was with your friend, Nancy?"

It took three tries, but she finally managed to get Kent's name out.

Taking Cody's hand and wrapping his other arm tightly around her shoulders, Logan half walked her, half dragged her, back to the far side of the display panels. The activities room was almost empty now. Only a few stragglers had lingered to talk.

"Kent?" Logan called across to him. "Kent, can you give us a hand here? Pronto?

"Robbie's disappeared," he said tersely when Kent reached them. "We've got to check the building fast Get Nancy to help, and anybody else who's still here. Search every room. I'll go check the look."

"I'll go with you, Dad," with Ms. Weyden

"No, Cody. I see it. Robbie crawled into a kid-and help. Hold her hand, okay? And stay right with her, because she's worried. She needs to have someone she knows with her.''

Ali looked down at Cody. The way her eyes were swimming, he was such a blur he might have been Robbie. That thought was enough to start her tears flowing.

"Hang in, Ali," Logan murmured, leaning closer. "We'll give this ten minutes, and if we haven't found him by then we'll call the police." Logan turned on his heel and started for the fire exit.

"Hey!" Kent called, attracting the attention of the few remaining people. "Folks, there's a little boy missing. If you can stay for just a few minutes and help us search the building, please do."

THE CLINIC was small enough that it had taken no time at all to establish Robbie wasn't anywhere inside. By then, Ali's control was all but gone.

"Come on, we'll go wait in my office," Nancy suggested.

Once they were there, Ali sat huddled on a chair, her entire body trembling. When Cody crawled onto her lap and began sobbing quietly against her shoulder, she wrapped her arms tightly around him and tried to force her mind to go blank. Her thoughts continued to swirl, though, tumbling over one another in a jumble of miraculo Logan was her last hope. Maybe he would find Robbie outside...

"It's going
But what if it w'ay," Nancy murmured.

find Robbie, and...al   ? What if Logan *didn't*
ing that she might never see   ldn't stop think-
                                       . She tried

to blink away fresh tears, then heard Logan in the hall. He strode into the office and silently shook his head. It made her heart feel as if steel bars were pressing in on it.

"I'm going to call the police now, all right?" he said.

She nodded wordlessly, but before he could reach for the phone on Nancy's desk, Kent appeared in the doorway.

"Ali? Someone's just called here asking for you."

"A man?" Logan demanded.

Kent shook his head. "I don't know. I didn't answer the phone. But somebody's waiting on the line for her."

"You can pick it up in here," Nancy told her.

Ali looked at the phone. One of its lights was flashing and she watched it blink for a moment, a new feeling of horror washing over her. The man who'd stolen Robbie was on that line. If she answered the phone, she'd hear his voice.

"It's him," she finally whispered. "It *has* to be him. Who else would be calling me here?"

Logan scooped Cody up off her lap.

"Answer it," he said when she didn't move.

wasn't going to happen. Not right now, at least. Right now, all he could do was try to help.

He waited another few seconds, then reached for the phone with his free hand and held it out to her. She was deathly pale, her hands shaking so badly he was afraid she'd drop the damned receiver if she *did* pick it up.

"Ali?" he murmured. "Ali, try to think calmly. It's *good* news that this guy's phoning you. In fact, it's terrific. He's getting in touch with you right away. That means he isn't just some wacko who goes around grabbing kids for no reason."

"Logan's right," Kent assured her.

"He wants something," Logan went on. "He wants something before he gives Robbie back. So I'm just going to keep holding the phone for you, and you're going to press that button, then pick up the receiver and find out what it is. *You* have to be the one to do that part."

He held his breath until she slowly and tentatively reached forward.

"You'll be fine," he whispered.

Terrified of what the man might say, Ali pushed the flashing button, then lifted the receiver and murmured, "Hello?"

"Hello, Ali," he said. "Don't say a word, but it's

she had

"Robbie   started her trembling so hard

police. I need   both hands.

you have you'll   call the

home now and wait for me to phone you there. *Don't* call the police. And don't tell anyone you've heard from me. You've got that?"

"Yes," she whispered.

"Good. Now—"

"No, wait! I've moved. You don't have the number. It's—"

"I've got it. Now go on home."

With a quiet click, the phone went dead against her ear. She simply sat holding the receiver, vainly trying to understand what was happening.

"Ali?" Nancy said.

"Who was it?" Logan asked.

"It was . . . my dead husband."

LOGAN SHOT a surreptitious glance at Ali as he drove the Cherokee along Harbord. She'd been in no shape to drive her own car home from the clinic, so she'd left it there. That, though, was the only suggestion she'd gone along with.

Nancy had wanted her to stay right where she was until the shock had worn off a little more, but Ali had been adamant about starting for home the moment Logan finished changing out of his Santa suit—saying she *had* to be home when her husband phoned again.

She'd also been adamant about swearing everyone to secrecy until she had Robbie safely back, even though both Nancy and Kent had argued that she should call the police. After all, they'd pointed out, regardless of Bob's being Robbie's father, this was a kidnapping. Logan could see their point, but he found it a lot easier to relate to Ali's.

"I've got to do exactly what Bob said," she'd insisted. "You're not even supposed to know it was him. I shouldn't have let it slip out, and you've got to swear not to breathe a word to anyone. We can't do *anything* that might cause trouble for Robbie. And that means no one calls the police."

Her only concern was getting her son back unharmed, just as Logan's would be under the same circumstance. But how long would that take? It would depend, he decided, on what it was the guy wanted her to do for him.

Logan turned south on Palmerston, wondering what on earth the story was with this Bob character. He didn't have a clue, but that was hardly surprising when even Ali didn't know what was happening. All he'd learned, by taking Kent aside for a minute, were the bare-boned details, that Bob Weyden had supposedly been murdered—about eighteen months ago—while on a business trip in Central America.

Obviously, though, the man wasn't dead. So maybe he'd actually just been held prisoner down there, or only been injured and spent the eighteen months recuperating. But neither of those possibilities would explain why he hadn't gotten in touch with Ali in a normal way. Why, instead, he'd pulled this stunt with Robbie.

Logan swung into her driveway and glanced at her again. "How're you doing?"

"Much better."

"And what—"

She silenced him with a shake of her head, then looked pointedly down at Cody who was half-asleep in her arms.

Logan nodded. She was right. The less they said in Cody's hearing the better. "You want some company for a while?" he asked.

"Would you mind?"

"'Course not." Cutting the engine and switching off the headlights, he climbed out into the night. It was clear and starry, but the air was so cold the snow squeaked beneath his feet.

He started around to the passenger's side, wishing he could think of a good way to explain things to his son. Cody was still awfully upset that Robbie was gone. And he'd picked up on just enough of the adult conversations to make him totally confused. It was too much for a six-year-old boy to understand. Hell, it was too much for a thirty-three-year-old man to understand.

"Come on, sport," he said, lifting Cody off Ali's lap. "We're going to go in with Ms. Weyden for a bit."

"And wait until the man brings Robbie home?"

"Well, we'll see. I'm not quite sure what the plans are for tonight. But we'll know what's happening by tomorrow." He followed Ali onto the porch, hoping to hell they would.

At least things weren't as bad as they'd first assumed. At least it hadn't been some deranged stranger who'd grabbed Robbie. And once the shock of hearing from a dead man had begun to wear off, Ali had clearly been relieved that Robbie was with his father.

"He'll be okay," she'd told Nancy and Kent when they'd insisted that she call the police. "Even though I'll worry every second until I've got him back, there's no way Bob would ever harm him."

Maybe she was right, but Logan wasn't entirely convinced. After all, what kind of a father played dead for a year and a half? What kind of man practically scared his wife to death by snatching their son? Once inside, Logan fixed Cody a peanut butter sandwich and sat with him at the kitchen table while Ali hovered by the phone.

"He's bound to call from a pay phone, isn't he?" she finally said. "Or a cell phone."

"Probably." Logan glanced at the phone on the counter, knowing exactly what she'd really been saying. She had a caller ID feature on her kitchen phone. The number from a pay phone wouldn't do them much good, though, and if Bob used a cell phone, only an Unknown would flash on the little screen.

Fortunately, Cody was too tired to ask any more questions, and by the time he finished his sandwich and a glass of milk he looked as if he was half-asleep again.

"Do you want to put him to bed upstairs?" Ali asked quietly.

Logan shook his head. At the moment, just the thought of letting Cody out of his sight was enough to make him break into a cold sweat. "How about waiting for your call in the living room, and he can curl up in there."

"Sure, I'll get a pillow and quilt."

"Ali?" Logan said as she turned to go upstairs.

"Yes?"

"Two things—just in case Bob phones before we have a chance to talk. First, he might ask if you told anyone *he* was your caller. If he does, tell him you didn't. There's no point in saying anything that could antagonize him."

"Oh, Logan, you don't really think he'll ask, do you? I'm not a very convincing liar."

"You don't have to be very good over the phone. And the other thing—tell him you'll *only* go along with whatever he wants on one condition. You get to talk to Robbie at least once a day."

Nodding, she turned away before Logan could see she was near tears again. *At least once a day.* That meant he thought Bob might not give Robbie back to her right away, when she could hardly stand to think about her son being gone another hour, let alone for days. And Logan hadn't spelled it out, but she knew he wanted her talking to Robbie every day so they'd be sure he was still alive.

She couldn't stand thinking about *that* at all.

WHILE LOGAN settled Cody on the love seat in front of the window, Ali sat on the couch, staring at the Christmas tree. It stood next to the fireplace, its lights flickering away, throwing tiny flashes of color onto the presents below.

The vast majority of those gifts were for Robbie, and seeing them there almost started her crying again. Christmas was for children, but her child was suddenly gone.

She pressed her fist to her mouth, trying to hold back the rush of pain that thought caused. Then she clicked on the end table's lamp, switching it to its dimmest setting so it wouldn't bother Cody, and got up to turn off the tree lights. Their cheerful twinkling was too depressing to bear.

When she sat down again she did her best to ignore both the tree and the stockings that already hung on the fireplace. *The stockings were hung by the chimney with care,* Robbie had quoted once they were in place. Remembering that made her throat ache even harder.

Forcing her eyes from the stockings, she focused on the mantel clock. But watching the minutes tick by, waiting for Bob's call, did nothing for her state of mind. As much as she didn't *really* believe he'd ever hurt his own son, what if...?

She told herself again that Robbie would be fine. She'd make certain he was by going along with whatever Bob wanted. And the more time she'd had to think, the more she suspected she knew what it was.

Only one possibility made any sense, and it also explained the previously inexplicable—why he'd increased his life insurance coverage so drastically, leaving her as the beneficiary even though they'd been separated.

Bob had faked his death, and now he was going to tell her to hand over the insurance money.

She'd give it to him, of course. To ensure Robbie's safety, she'd do anything. But how long would it take to turn her investments back into cash? Surely not more than a day. So despite what Logan had implied, she could get Robbie back tomorrow. If she called first thing in the morning... but what if Kent Schiraldi caused a problem?

Suddenly, she wished she'd hired a stranger to help her invest the policy proceeds. Since Kent knew what had happened to Robbie, he'd realize why she wanted the money. He'd have a fit, probably start insisting again that she call the police, and if *anything* went wrong in all this... A few stray tears made good their escape. She brushed them away as Logan headed across the room.

"Cody's asleep," he said, sinking onto the couch beside her. "So you want to talk?"

She hesitated, half wanting to confide in him, half not. "I haven't really been able to make much sense of things yet," she said at last.

"Hey, I write crime fiction, remember? If I knew the whole story, maybe I could help you figure out what's going on. Ali?" he added after a few seconds. "Next to Cody, Robbie's my favorite kid in the world. So let me try to help, huh?"

"All right," she said slowly. When he put it that way, how could she shut him out? But he *did* need to know the whole story to understand how things had gotten to where they were, which meant she had to start way back.

"I guess," she began, "the first thing I should explain is that Bob and I..." Pausing, she tried to decide if there were *some* details she could leave out. She really hated admitting what a fool she'd once been.

"Kent told me your husband was supposedly killed in Central America," Logan prompted. "About a year and a half ago."

"Yes. It happened...I mean it *supposedly* happened, in Nicaragua. And did he tell you Bob and I were separated at the time?"

"No."

"Well, we were—permanently. I mean, a legal separation agreement, the whole thing." Ali slowly pushed her hair back from her face, a gesture that told Logan she was feeling uncomfortable with the topic.

"That happened," she went on at last, "a couple of years before Bob was killed...supposedly killed. We'd talked about a divorce, but neither of us had filed. Not me, because I wasn't even *seeing* anyone else, so there didn't seem to be any point bothering about it. Not Bob, because...well, that isn't really relevant to the story."

"Ahh," Logan said, for lack of anything better. So she'd never exactly been a grieving widow after all. It made him wonder what might have happened between them if he'd known that when they'd first met, if he hadn't spent the past year biding his time. He forced the question from his mind as she continued.

"I know I kind of gave people the wrong impression when I moved here," she said quietly. "By just saying I was a widow, I mean."

"Well...yes, kind of."

"It was the truth, though. At least I thought it was until tonight. And it was easier for me not to mention the separated part."

"I guess that sort of thing isn't really anybody else's business, is it."

"No... but that's not why I left it out. It was because, before, whenever I had to explain that my marriage had broken up, I'd always felt like a failure. I know that sounds silly in the nineties, but you understand what I mean?"

"Yeah... yeah, I do. After my wife told me she wanted a divorce, I had the same feeling, even though... Well, there's nothing rational about it, is there. Relationships just don't always work."

She gave him a tiny smile that started a tingling in his groin—which made him feel like a total jerk. Right now, when it came to emotional control, Ali had to be hanging on by her fingernails. So he should be giving all his attention to her problem. This was neither the time nor place to be thinking about how kissable that wan little smile made her look.

"My parents separated when I was little," she was saying. "I almost never saw my father while I was growing up. Now I'm lucky if I ever hear from him. At any rate, I always said I'd do whatever it took to make *my* marriage work when the time came. But then it *didn't* work, and Robbie didn't see any more of Bob than I did of my father. Ironic, isn't it."

"Like I said, relationships just don't always work."

"I guess. And it's obvious now that Bob and I should never have gotten married in the first place. I was too young—only twenty—and he was almost forty."

"A cradle-robber."

"That's exactly what my mother called him. Oh, Logan, if she was still alive...if she knew what he'd done tonight...she told me I was making a big mistake, but I wouldn't listen."

"*Nobody* listens to their parents when they're twenty. We'll have to remember that when Robbie and Cody are older."

Ali's eyes filled with tears, making Logan wish he'd bitten his tongue before the words slipped out. She didn't start crying, though, just wiped her eyes and continued.

"Compared to anyone else I'd ever dated, Bob was a mature, successful man. At least, that's how I saw him at the time. And I was bored with my classes and so darned flattered that someone like him was interested in me. So instead of going back to university for my final undergraduate year... You're right, you know, Logan. There are a lot of things we should remember for when the boys are older. I was so dumb. I could be a practicing psychologist right now. Instead, I'm not even in grad school yet. But the bottom line is that I should have known better than to marry Bob."

"If he was almost forty, I'd say he's the one who should have known better."

She managed another tiny smile. "What I meant by *my* knowing better, was that I knew Bob's first wife walked out on him. And if I hadn't been so naive, I'd have realized he was marrying me partly to prove a point. But that's all water under the bridge. Tonight, though...taking Robbie the way he did...oh, Logan, he *should* have known better than to do that."

This time, she *did* begin crying, and if Logan had ever been with a woman who desperately needed a hug, it was her. He pulled her close, wishing he could shut out the world with his arms. She felt incredibly soft and warm, and she smelled of the craziest combination of scents imaginable—chocolate chip cookies and forbidden desire.

He tried to ignore it, but it was so tantalizing, that was impossible. So then he tried telling himself he was being absurd. Desire wasn't a scent. But there was something about being close to Ali that turned on *all* his senses.

"I'm sorry," she finally said, drawing away and digging some tissues from her pocket. "I *am* sure that Robbie will be safe with Bob, so crying is—"

Tensing, she stopped midsentence when the phone in the kitchen rang.

Chapter Three

Ali reached the phone by the third ring, Logan on her heels. Even though she'd expected it, seeing the little Unknown flashing on the screen sent a stab of disappointment through her. She grabbed the phone from the counter and said hello before she had the receiver halfway to her ear.

"Let me talk to Robbie," she demanded the moment she heard Bob's voice.

"I can't," he said. "He's not with me."

"What?" Her heart began beating triple time. "What do you mean, he's not with you?"

"You think it was *me* who took him?"

"Of course that's what I think! Are you saying it wasn't?"

"Hell, Ali, I'm not heartless."

Her knees were suddenly weak and her head was spinning. She leaned against the wall for support. A *stranger* had her son after all!

Hysteria rushed over her like a giant wave, but just as the undertow began sweeping her away, Logan rested his hand on her arm and whispered that she had to stay in control.

"Bob," she managed to say after a moment, "I don't understand. When you phoned before, you said Robbie was with you."

"No, I said he's safe. And that once you do what I tell you, you'll get him back."

"It's the insurance money you want, isn't it?"

"Yes."

"Well you can have it, but what about Robbie? Where—"

"Ali, he'll be fine. And I'll let you talk to him tomorrow. But I don't think either of us would want him knowing I'm alive. Not when I'm just going to disappear again."

"But, I—"

"Look, as soon as you give me the money, I'll be out of your life for good. Robbie's, too. So don't you figure it's better for him to just keep on believing I'm dead? Him and everyone else, too?"

She took a deep breath, trying to think far enough through her fear and confusion to decide *what* was better.

As long as she'd known Bob, his first and foremost concern had been about what would be best for *him*. So was he really thinking of Robbie's welfare now, or did he have a hidden agenda? He'd arranged for someone else to take Robbie. Some stranger. Which meant Robbie was probably terrified, and that sure didn't add up to Bob's being concerned.

But in a perverse way he was making sense. Maybe, in the long run, it *would* be better if Robbie went on believing his father was dead. Assuming there was going to *be* a long run. Thinking about the possibility there wouldn't be started her stomach knotting.

"All right," she finally murmured. "All right, then, you're doing what you think is best. But at least tell me who he's with."

"Ali, he's safe. That's all you need to know. He's my son, too, and I don't want him hurt. I just had to make sure you wouldn't give me any hassles."

Covering the receiver with her hand, she shook her head at Logan, trying to tell him she was in trouble. Her throat was so tight she wasn't certain she could say another word, let alone continue this conversation.

There was something going on that Bob wasn't mentioning. And he could tell her he didn't want Robbie hurt from here to China, but that didn't guarantee a damned thing when Robbie wasn't even with him.

Logan rested his hands firmly on her shoulders, giving them an encouraging squeeze. "Just take it easy," he whispered. "You're doing fine. But has he agreed to let you talk to Robbie?"

"Bob, listen to me," she finally said, forcing herself to go on. "I'll get you the money, but what if I can't get it tomorrow? It's invested and the broker will have to—"

"Get it fast, Ali. The faster you do that, the faster you get Robbie back."

"Bob... Bob, I don't know how you can be doing this. Not this way. It's about the worst thing you could possibly have done. And... and if it does take me longer than just tomorrow, I want you to promise I can talk to Robbie the next day, too. Every day he's not home."

There was a long silence at the other end of the line. She listened to the hammering of her heart and waited.

"All right," Bob said at last. "But only as long as you don't try anything dumb. You don't ask him any questions. Nothing like where is he or who's he with. One question like that and it's the last call. You understand?"

"Yes. Perfectly."

"Okay, then. I'll set things up for a little before nine tomorrow morning. And I'll phone you again myself, right after that, to give you instructions about the money. Wait until you've heard from me before you call that broker. And listen, you did what I told you before? You didn't tell anyone at the clinic it was me who called, did you?"

"No, nobody. I said I didn't recognize the voice."

"Good, make sure you stick to that. And remember what I said about no police. I'll know if you contact them, Ali. I'll know."

With that, the line went dead.

LOGAN CHECKED ON CODY, who was still fast asleep in the living room, then went back to the kitchen and stood waiting for the coffee to finish perking, giving Ali a few more minutes to pull herself together.

She'd managed to tell him that Bob had agreed to let her talk to Robbie every morning, but she'd been so close to tears when she'd hung up that she hadn't been able to discuss the rest of the conversation right away.

Hearing her half, though, had given Logan a pretty good idea of what was what.

"Insurance money," she'd said. That's what Bob wanted from her. But how the hell much money did it take to make a guy snatch his own son?

The coffeemaker began sputtering, so he grabbed a couple of mugs. While he was filling them, Ali wandered over from where she'd been standing by the stove.

"When I hear from Robbie," she said, her voice a little uneven, "he's going to be on a cell phone, too. Bob will make sure of that, so there's no point even hoping we'll get a number."

"No...there probably isn't." He handed her a mug, leaned against the counter and waited for her to go on. "You feel up to telling me the rest of the details yet?" he prompted when she didn't.

"I . . . I think so."

"Okay, do your best to remember everything Bob said."

She took a sip of coffee, then put it down and started with his "Hello."

Logan saved his questions for later and just listened while she repeated the conversation.

"And right before he hung up," she concluded, "he told me that if I contacted the police, he'd know. That was the last thing he said."

"He was just trying to intimidate you," Logan said—more to make her feel better than because he believed it. All Bob had to do was have somebody watching her, and he'd know if she went to the police or if they came to the house.

"Well, his intimidation worked," she murmured. "Oh, Logan, I'm really scared."

"Ali...we're going to make this turn out okay."

She nodded, but her face was pale and her dark eyes were filled with tears.

It had been a long, long time since anyone except Cody had stirred protective feelings in him, but right now he desperately wanted to keep Ali from being afraid. That wasn't an available option, though. So instead, he mentally ran through everything she'd just told him.

If tonight had been a chapter in one of his books, he'd have written a clue into Bob's dialogue—had him say something that would have sent them racing out into the darkness, knowing exactly where they'd find Robbie.

But this was real life, and things were far from that simple. Robbie was *somewhere* in a city of four million people, and Bob hadn't given them even the slightest hint where.

"This insurance money Bob wants," he said at last. "It's a payment you got because he was supposedly dead?"

Ali nodded.

"And how much are we talking?"

She hesitated, then said, "You're going to find this hard to believe, but two million dollars."

"Jeez," he muttered, "that was quite some policy. And you've got the money invested in what?"

"Mutual funds. Kent looked after everything for me—he's a financial adviser. So I'll call him first thing in the morning. And if he sells right away... it won't take much time to free up the money, will it?''

Logan swore silently.

"Will it?'' she repeated.

"I think—no, I don't *think*, I know. It takes five working days to get your money out of anything like that. The time's set by the Securities Commission.''

"Five days?'' she whispered, her face turning an even paler shade of white. "Oh, no, Logan, you must be wrong.''

"I wish I was, but...Ali, you can check one of your statements. It'll say that right on it someplace.''

"But five days would be until Friday. Robbie can't be gone for *five* more days. What if...'' She stopped speaking and tears began streaming down her face.

Logan put his coffee onto the counter and reached for her, wrapping his arms around her and holding her while she cried. Once again, he could smell the crazy scent that made him think of chocolate chip cookies and forbidden desire. Not knowing what else he could do, he simply stroked her hair until she finally stopped sobbing.

"It has to be such a traumatic thing for him,'' she whispered at last. "He won't know why he's with a stranger, why he isn't home with me. Logan, that kind of experience can shatter a child. What if the psychological damage...''

"Shhh,'' he murmured, "that's not going to happen. He's a well-adjusted little guy, and he'll come through just fine. You'll see.''

"Oh, I hope so. I only hope...I'll be back in a minute,'' she said, moving out of his embrace. "I'm

just going upstairs...need to wash my face and...I'll
be back in a minute."

He sank onto a chair once she'd left the kitchen,
trying not to dwell on the issue of how this might af-
fect Robbie. They'd worry about that once they had
him back.

But Ali was right. It didn't take a degree in psychology to realize the potential for damage. And the
longer Robbie was gone...well, they had to get him
back as soon as they could.

Of course, the decision on how to play this had to
be Ali's, but he had a gut feeling she shouldn't just sit
back, go along with what Bob wanted and assume
everything would come up roses.

All he needed was a brilliant idea about what she
should do.

IT WAS A GOOD HALF HOUR before Ali reappeared
downstairs, and Logan's gut feeling that they should
be actively doing *something* had been growing
stronger the entire time she'd been gone. She poured
herself fresh coffee, then slid into the chair across the
table from him, looking like death warmed over.

"Feel any better?" he asked.

"A little. I...I checked the fund statements and you
were right about the five days. So I guess I just have
to keep telling myself that, no matter how long this
takes, Bob would never let anyone hurt his own son."

Logan fleetingly wondered if she was *really* sure of
that, but he refrained from asking.

"You know how long five days can be for a little
boy, though," she continued. "And he's got to be

awfully frightened. So don't you think Kent should be able to speed up the process somehow? Get my money faster?''

"No. . . no, we're going to be stuck with playing by the rules.''

"But there *must* be a way.''

Raking his fingers through his hair, Logan tried to decide what to say. Since her husband wasn't really dead, she should never have gotten that insurance money in the first place. And now, legally, she was required to pay it back—not hand it over to Bob.

That obviously hadn't occurred to her, but it sure would occur to Kent, and if she asked him for the money he'd have no choice but to tell the insurance company what was going on. If he didn't, he'd be making himself a party to fraud and putting his entire career at risk. But as soon as he opened his mouth the police would get involved.

"Surely,'' Ali was saying, "if Kent told whoever's in charge how *urgently* I need the money. . .''

"Ali . . . look, if you want the money we're going to have to circumvent Kent.''

"Why?''

"Because he'd know you wanted it for Bob, so you'd be asking him to bend his ethics totally out of shape. But who do your statements come from? The brokerage house he bought the funds through?''

She nodded.

"Good. Then you can bypass him by calling them directly. You can just say you're looking after your own investments now, but you *can't* say that you need two million bucks *urgently,* to pay a kidnapper.

Somebody'd call the cops for sure—figure they were obliged to. So unless we decide we want to involve the police after all . . ."

Logan could tell Ali was about to start crying once more, so he hurried on. "Let's consider a different angle. I've been thinking there might be some way, some sort of deal we could make with Bob, that would get Robbie back faster."

"What sort of deal?" She gazed at him with a faint glimmer of hope in her eyes.

"I'm not exactly sure, but if we could come up with an idea before you talk to him again . . ."

Ali wrapped her fingers around the warmth of her mug, telling herself that if Logan thought they might be able to play "Let's Make a Deal" with Bob, then the most useful thing she could do was concentrate on thinking about that. She had to try to stop focusing on her worries about Robbie.

"Let's run through what we know," Logan suggested. "See if anything leaps out at us."

"All right."

"Okay, square one is that Bob was supposed to be dead, but he's not. And he wants that money, so he takes Robbie to make you hand it over. And—"

"And someone helped him."

"Yeah, you mentioned that part. He doesn't want Robbie to know he's really still alive, so he got someone else to—"

"No, I didn't mean whoever he got to *physically* take Robbie. I meant that somebody who knows *me* helped him."

Logan looked at her curiously. "If you're right, that puts a whole new twist on things. But why are you thinking that?"

"Because of everything Bob knew. I've been so upset that I only realized it while I was upstairs, but somebody must have told him I was taking Robbie to that party. And when I said I'd moved here, he already knew. He had my number, even though it's unlisted. Logan, there *has* to be somebody else involved."

He sat rubbing his jaw for a minute, then said, "Finding out where you're living, or even getting the phone number, wouldn't have been tough. And I just assumed Bob had been watching the house and followed you to the clinic. But, you know, that snatch was so damned smooth maybe he *couldn't* have set it up on the spur of the moment."

"You think I'm right, then?"

"I think you might be. Who do you figure it was?"

She took a deep breath. She didn't know where this was going to get them, but at least Logan hadn't laughed at her suspicions. "I think there's only one person it could be. His name's Vinny Velarde, and he was Bob's business partner."

"And he knew Robbie would be at the party?"

"Yes, he called the other day and I mentioned it. He's not my favorite person, but he keeps in touch—says he likes to know how Robbie's doing. But maybe it's actually that he and Bob..."

"Okay, let's develop that scenario a little. Bob decides he's going to take Robbie, and he gets this Vinny to check out a good time."

"Vinny might even have been the man Cody saw," Ali said. "That would explain why Robbie didn't yell or anything. He'd have gone with Vinny if he'd thought there was some reason to."

Logan nodded. "Okay, so it's possible Vinny was the man. But even if he wasn't, if he's been feeding Bob information, then he knew Bob wasn't dead. So does that mean Vinny's been in on things right from the beginning? You'd better fill in some of the background for me."

"I...oh, Logan, it's all so complicated that I don't know where to start."

"Just pick a place. If I get confused, I'll tell you."

She thought for a minute, then said, "All right, I'll start with the insurance money, explain why the policy—no, I should start back further, with Bob's murder."

"Which never actually happened."

"Apparently not." She took a sip of coffee and did her best to organize the facts in her head. "All right," she finally said, "keep in mind that Bob and I were separated, so all I know is what Vinny told me. That and the odd thing the insurance people said."

Logan nodded.

"All right, then. Bob went to Nicaragua about eighteen months ago, on some sort of business trip. He and Vinny had an import-export business, called Custom Cargoes, which Vinny still owns. According to him, Bob made the trip to set up a link with an exporter there. But I gather the RCMP thought—"

"Wait a minute," Logan interrupted. "The RCMP? Why did the feds get involved if this imaginary murder happened in Nicaragua?"

She hesitated. Even after all this time, it was embarrassing to admit she'd married Bob without even suspecting he sometimes wandered onto the shady side of the law. But if she was going to tell Logan the facts, there was no way around telling him all of them.

"Ali?"

"Yes, I'm just deciding how to simplify this so it doesn't take forever. The RCMP got involved because they were suspicious about what Bob was importing. And maybe they were right to be—no, *probably* they were right to be. After Bob and I had been married for a while, I began to think there had to be two sides to Custom Cargoes—and that one of them was anything but legitimate."

"You began to *think,*" Logan said. "Did you ever find out for sure?"

"No, but my best guess is that they'd been running illegal alcohol into Canada for years. A while after Bob and I had called it quits, I know the RCMP were checking Custom Cargoes out. They talked to me— thought I'd know more than I actually did. But neither Bob nor Vinny were ever charged, so there couldn't have been enough evidence."

"But what about Nicaragua? Why were the RCMP interested in what happened there?"

"I think they figured Bob's trip had something to do with expanding the business. Or diversifying— however you'd put it. There was probably a drug connection down there. Or guns, maybe. Everything seemed to add up to that. Bob was making a deal, it went sour, so he ended up dead. Which explained the finger, too. I mean, it's the sort of thing drug dealers or guerrillas would do to make a statement, isn't it."

"The finger?"

"Oh . . . Kent didn't tell you about that?"

Logan shook his head.

"Oh." She hesitated again, this time because she felt queasy. "Somebody," she made herself continue, "mailed Bob's little finger to Vinny."

Chapter Four

"I will, Nancy," Ali said, gesturing to Logan that she was having trouble getting off the phone. "I'll call you tomorrow. No, I'm really not a basket case yet, not quite... I know, if there's anything at all I need..."

Logan dumped the lukewarm remains of the coffee from the mugs, poured fresh refills and carried them back to the table, thinking Nancy McGuire just might have the worst timing in the entire world.

He could understand her wanting to know if Ali had heard from Bob again, but he wished she hadn't called at the exact second Ali's *finger* line was hanging fire.

"*Somebody,*" she'd said, "mailed Bob's little finger to Vinny."

But had it really been Bob's? It must have been, he decided. The RCMP would have checked that out, and it wouldn't have taken more than two seconds for a forensic lab to determine whether or not it was his. So unless he was adding something up very wrong, Bob had intentionally faked his death—and had chopped off his finger and mailed it to his partner as proof.

Logan slowly shook his head. Old Bob was sounding weirder than a lot of the fictional characters he dreamed up, and he wanted to get to the rest of the details. He waved at Ali, moving his hand in the circular motion that film directors use to speed things up.

Film directors ... L.A. He absently realized that since Robbie had vanished he hadn't thought once about his move to L.A. Before that, he'd been thinking of virtually nothing else.

Ali impatiently drummed her fingers against the counter until she finally managed to grab an opening for a goodbye. When she hung up she was almost wishing Nancy hadn't called. Talking about Robbie had brought all her fears about his safety to the fore again.

She did a little deep breathing on her way back to the table, reminding herself she was doing the most constructive thing she could. If she and Logan were able to make complete sense of the situation, she'd be in a better position to negotiate with Bob.

"Where was I?" she asked, sitting down across from Logan once more.

"The finger. You said somebody mailed it to Vinny. You meant from Nicaragua?"

"Yes. And there was a note with it, saying double-dealers don't live long there."

"And the note was from ... ?"

She shrugged. "Vinny claimed he had no idea. Not about who it was from, not about what it meant. He swore Custom Cargoes' business down there was legitimate, and he stuck to that. At any rate, when Vinny got the finger he called the police and ..."

"And?"

"No, there's no reason to waste time on all that. I only need to tell you about the insurance. Both Bob and Vinny had business insurance policies, so Custom Cargoes wouldn't be at risk of going under if one of the partners suddenly died."

"That's pretty standard," Logan said.

"I know. But what *wasn't* standard was the value of the policies. There was five million dollars' coverage on each of them."

Logan gave a low whistle and Ali shrugged again. "I guess they wanted it high because the shady side of the business was risky."

"I guess," Logan agreed. "So if Bob died, the business would get five million and you'd get two, from the personal policy. And were both policies with the same insurance company?"

"Uh-huh."

"Well, I'll bet hearing he'd been killed made *their* day. But since he's not *really* dead, there couldn't have been a body. So you're saying they paid out all that money without one?"

Ali nodded.

"That's tough to believe."

"It gets even tougher when you hear the rest."

"I can hardly wait."

"Well, the personal insurance wasn't originally worth anything like two million. And it was immediately before the trip to Nicaragua that Bob increased it."

"You're right. It *is* getting tougher to believe."

"I know. The insurance people were really suspicious. Vinny told them that Bob had figured Central

America was a dangerous place to be going, which sort of explained his upping the value. But what I never understood was why Bob had left *me* as the beneficiary. I wasn't exactly his favorite person after we'd broken up, so I thought he'd have changed that. His mother is still alive. Or he could have named Robbie. After tonight, though, I think I see what he was up to."

Logan sat silently for a minute, then said, "If he'd died with Robbie as his beneficiary, the money would have had to go into a trust. Until Robbie's an adult."

"Exactly. It's all starting to come together now, isn't it. If Bob planned this whole thing as an insurance scam, he'd want *me* to have the money because it would be easy to make me hand it over. All he had to do was...was exactly what he did." Her eyes suddenly filled with tears and she blinked hard.

"You want to take a break from this?" Logan asked quietly.

She shook her head. "I want to get it entirely figured out."

"All right," he said after a minute, "then tell me this. If that finger and note were the only so-called proof of death, why did the insurance company pay out seven million bucks?"

"Well, at first they refused to. But Vinny wasn't giving up without a fight, so he flew to Nicaragua to see what he could find out down there."

"And he obviously found something good."

"Supposedly. Although now I'm wondering whether he found it or bought it. At any rate, he came back with a sworn statement from a senior police official. I never saw it—well, it was in Spanish, anyway. But it said that Bob had been reported as missing by the fellow he'd gone down to meet with. The man was an important local, so the police investigated. That led to a tip about a body buried in the jungle." She paused, feeling queasy once more.

"And they identified the body as Bob's," Logan concluded.

"Yes. The story was that his ID was on it . . . and it was missing the little finger."

"But didn't the insurance company ask them to ship it up here? So they could have it examined themselves?"

"It disappeared."

"What?"

Ali shrugged. "I don't know, Logan, Vinny was the one down there."

"And you think he might have helped arrange for it to conveniently disappear? So the insurance company couldn't have it examined?"

"Maybe. Or maybe there was never really any body in the first place. I just don't know."

"Incredible. So they paid the claims mainly on the statement Vinny got."

"Yes. It took a while, but I guess they finally decided Vinny's story was likely to hold up in court."

"Because nobody would ever suspect a police official in Central America of taking a bribe," Logan muttered. "What a joke. But that all took time. When did you actually get the money?"

"Not until a couple of weeks ago."

"Then Bob turns up fast—before you have a chance to spend any of it."

"I'd never have spent any of it," she said quietly. "When Bob and I separated, our agreement gave me the house we'd lived in. It was one of those enormous old things in Rosedale and—well, I sold it after he'd...disappeared. That gave me enough money to buy here and go back to school. But I'd never have touched the insurance money. That just wouldn't have felt right, somehow, so I invested it for Robbie.

"It's ironic, isn't it," she continued after a moment. "Now I'll be using it to get Robbie back. But the money doesn't matter. All I care about is getting him home safely."

"I know. I know, and you will. Everything's going to turn out just fine."

Ali smiled a little, making Logan glad he'd said that—even though hearing the story hadn't prompted a single brilliant idea about what they should do. He rubbed his jaw, hoping he looked thoughtful rather than uncertain, but he knew they needed help with this.

"Look," he said at last, "I've got a friend named Wes Penna who's a private investigator. If it's okay with you, I'd like to call him—tell him about all this and see what he thinks."

Ali didn't look exactly happy with the suggestion. "We can trust him not to say anything to anyone else?"

"Absolutely."

"Well...I guess. Do you want to do it right now?"

"No, I don't have his number with me." He hesitated. It was getting late, but he didn't like the idea of
leaving Ali on her own. What if old Bob took it into
his head to phone in the middle of the night or something?

"You know," he finally said, "maybe I should go
home, grab a few things and come back. Cody and I
could spend the night here so you aren't all alone. Sort
of moral support."

He thought she'd say no, but she didn't. "You're
sure you wouldn't mind?" she asked quietly.

"Positive." Shoving himself up from the table, he
started for the hall, saying, "I'll be back in a few
minutes."

He took a quick look into the living room at Cody,
then grabbed his jacket from the coat tree and headed
out into the cold.

ON THE WAY to his place from Ali's, Logan decided
he'd call Wes *before* he went back. That way, he could
ask whatever questions he wanted to without running
the risk of making her even more worried.

He unlocked his front door and started straight for
the kitchen, ignoring the trail of snowy footprints he
was leaving in his wake. Ignoring Sammy, though, was
a different story. The moment the cat heard the key in
the lock he was on his way downstairs, loudly calling
his resentment about having been left alone.

Once they reached the kitchen, the cat switched to
complaining about being on the brink of starvation.
And when Logan grabbed his address book first, instead of the empty cat food bowl, Sammy pointed out

the error in no uncertain terms by wrapping himself around Logan's ankles and meowing piteously while Logan flipped through the pages to find Wes's number.

The cordless phone in his hand, Logan punched in the number, then grabbed the box of cat food from the cupboard and poured some in a bowl. That brought forth more yowls, these intended to inform everyone within two blocks that Sammy much preferred canned food over dry.

"It's been a tough night for all of us, Sam," Logan muttered, just as someone picked up at Wes's house.

It turned out that Wes was on the East Coast. He'd gone to Halifax on a case. Fortunately, though, his wife had the number of his hotel. Once Logan reached him, he summarized the facts as quickly and concisely as he could. When he was done, Wes asked several questions, then fell silent.

"Well?" Logan finally said. "What do you think?"

"I'm just wondering why she's so sure the kid's going to be safe. This guy doesn't exactly sound like father of the year."

An uneasy feeling settled in the pit of Logan's stomach. He'd had that exact thought himself—more than once.

"She didn't really say *why*," he told Wes. "Maybe it's just what she *wants* to believe."

"Yeah, well, I sure wouldn't count on him worrying about what happens to anyone but himself. And frankly, I don't like the sound of anything about this."

That sent the uneasy feeling spreading through Logan's entire body.

"You're talking about a guy," Wes went on, "who's put one helluva lot of effort into making people think he's dead. And for someone to go to such extremes...well, it strikes me as maybe *too* much just for money. I think there must have been something else driving him."

"It's a *lot* of money, Wes."

"Not to a guy who's been running contraband booze for years. And since that's a major area of organized crime, I'm wondering if somebody wanted him seriously dead."

"Ahh, you don't think you're kind of reaching?"

"Uh-uh. If the RCMP investigated him, he wasn't small potatoes. Which means he had to have been playing with the big boys. And he only had to cross the wrong guy once. So if that's what happened, scamming the insurance company wasn't his main reason for going to ground. He hid out to save his skin. But now he wants the money for spending cash while he's setting himself up in a new life."

"So what the hell do Ali and I do? Call the police? Give Bob the money?"

"There's no cut-and-dried answer. You'll have to make a judgment call, based on what you know."

"Dammit, Wes, what I know is *fictional* crime. You know real life. What would you do?"

Wes hesitated, finally saying, "Well, as far as the cops go, if you involve them, your guy's likely to find out and...well, they *might* come up with something, but they don't have a real good track record for getting kidnap victims back alive."

"So you're saying we shouldn't call them."

"No, I'm not. Logan, I *can't* advise you not to call the cops. Not if I want to keep my license."

"Okay, I hear what you aren't saying."

"Good. And as for your friend handing over the money, if she does, she'll be making herself an accomplice to insurance fraud."

"Yeah, that already occurred to me. But I can't imagine even an insurance company prosecuting her under the circumstances."

"Maybe not, but I'd lay odds they'd do their damnedest to get their hands on any assets she has—restitution for at least some of their loss."

"Well, right now, that would be the last thing Ali would worry about. So if giving Bob his money is the best way..."

"I didn't say that, either, Logan. I said you'll have to weigh the alternatives. I mean, he gets his money and then what? After all the trouble he's gone to, to convince people he's dead, you figure he'll want to leave anyone around who knows he's really alive?"

Logan closed his eyes and tried to force away the image of Ali and Robbie lying dead.

THE EXTERIOR of almost every house on Palmerston was decorated for Christmas. Colored lights sparkled in the cold night, strung among tree branches and outlining windows and roof lines. Santa's entire team of reindeer pranced in a floodlit front yard across the street. Logan was vaguely aware of the displays as he walked back to Ali's, but he doubted all the holiday cheer in the entire city would have done anything to lighten his mood.

Ali was a gutsy lady, but she'd already had a horrendous night. That tempted him to leave telling her about his conversation with Wes until morning. Or, at the very least, to minimize Wes's concerns. But the sooner they made some decisions the better. And they weren't going to make the best ones if he glossed things over. This wasn't, he reminded himself, one of his books. This was real life for two people he cared about a lot—maybe even a lot more than he'd realized.

Real life. And, if Wes was right, possibly real death. Thinking of that again sent a shiver through him that had nothing to do with the frosty air.

He climbed the porch steps and opened the front door, without even thinking that Ali might not have left it unlocked for him. Then it struck him that maybe she shouldn't have. In this part of Toronto, he'd never normally have a concern like that, but tonight...

"I'm back," he called quietly, and felt relieved when she replied.

He tugged off his cowboy boots, then clicked the dead bolt into place. Not that it would do much good if someone really wanted in. The upper halves of the old front doors in the neighborhood were almost entirely glass, which had been fine back in the 1890s when the houses were built. But this was the 1990s.

Almost no one, though, had replaced the old doors. And not a single neighbor had ever installed bars over the glass. Palmerston was a safe street in a safe city. So, he decided, hanging up his jacket and heading down the hall, it was only the events of the night that had his nerves on edge.

In the living room, Cody was still curled up on the love seat, under his quilt, and Ali was sitting on the couch. Dim light from a single lamp was highlighting golden strands of her hair.

"I put some towels in the guest room," she told him as he sank down beside her. "But I didn't bother changing Robbie's bed for Cody. I thought you'd probably feel better if he slept with you tonight."

He nodded. It might be silly, but she was right.

"I was just sitting here watching him," she continued quietly. "Just thinking that if I'd been watching Robbie more carefully at the party..."

"Oh, Ali," he murmured, brushing away the tear trickling down her cheek. "Ali, don't. It wasn't your fault. You're the best mother I know."

"Then why is my son gone?" she whispered, fiercely wiping away more tears.

"Because of Bob. Not because of you." He inched closer to her and draped his arm around her shoulders. She buried her face against him. The fresh-meadow scent of her hair made him forget it was winter and think of spring.

After a few moments she straightened up and gave him the most dismal attempt at a smile he'd ever seen. "You were gone longer than I expected. I was starting to worry."

"Sorry. I took time to call Wes Penna."

"And he said...?"

"Well, he said quite a bit. You're going to find some of it upsetting, but I'm going to be perfectly straight with you—so we can decide what's best to do, okay?"

"Okay," she murmured.

He started in, wishing to hell Wes had said even one or two things that sounded encouraging. But it all seemed even more pessimistic than it had originally.

When he got to Wes's suspicions that Bob had faked his death because he was on the run from the mob, Ali merely nodded, as if she figured that was a good guess. In fact, she was taking everything he told her surprisingly calmly. Then he realized that wasn't really true. The longer he talked the paler she grew. By the time he was almost done, he was thinking again about not mentioning Wes's most serious concern until the morning. But he pressed on, knowing he should get everything on the table at once.

"What it seems to boil down to," he concluded, "is that calling the police would be risky. And Wes didn't sound like he had a lot of faith in what they'd be able to do."

"I think," Ali murmured, "that I'd have been too terrified to call them, anyway, even if he'd said we should. I'd have been so scared that Bob would find out and...oh, I just don't know what he'd do if I crossed him. Maybe take off with Robbie and never let me see him again."

Or maybe, Logan thought, something even worse—whether she crossed him or not.

"So," she said, "Wes thought the best thing to do was just go ahead and give Bob the money?"

Logan cleared his throat. They'd reached show time and he didn't feel up to it.

She waited, watching him evenly.

"Wes saw a problem with just handing over the money, too," he said at last. "He thinks that after

Bob's gone to so much trouble to make people think he's dead—well, Wes doesn't figure he'll want to leave anyone around who knows he's really alive. Once he's got the money..."

Ali simply continued to gaze at Logan for a moment, then she pressed her fingers to her mouth, whispering, "Oh, my Lord. Oh, my Lord, you don't *really* think he could be right about that, do you?"

She'd begun to tremble, so Logan drew her close and held her. She felt so good against him that he couldn't help wishing the circumstances were entirely different—for selfish reasons, as well as for her sake and Robbie's. He'd like her to be in his arms because it was where she wanted to be, not simply because she needed comforting.

He pushed those thoughts away. The circumstances *weren't* different. And until they were...hell, there was no point in thinking about *until*, either. Because even if this all turned out just fine, he'd be on his way to L.A. in a few weeks.

Eventually, Ali drew back and looked at him again. "We've been forgetting something. Bob probably *wouldn't* want to leave anyone around who knows he's really alive, but Robbie isn't going to know. Bob said it would be better for him just to go on believing his father was dead, remember?"

"But *you'll* know," Logan said quietly.

"Yes...yes, I will. But once Bob has the money he'll be in a hurry to get away from Toronto. So I don't think I have *too* much to worry about. And as long as Robbie's safe..."

Logan didn't want to say another word, but he forced himself to. "When it comes down to even Robbie's safety, are you absolutely *sure* you can trust Bob?"

Her eyes luminous, she murmured, "No."

"No," he repeated quietly, relieved that she'd stopped trying to delude herself. "Then we can't go merrily along with him. You can't give him the money unless you get Robbie back first. You'll have to—"

"No, I'm not going to have the slightest say in the arrangements, Logan. And I know there won't be any chance of getting Robbie back before Bob has his money. He doesn't trust people at all, me included, so he'd never just agree to... I'd have to have some bargaining power and I don't. I've been thinking and thinking, but I can't come up with *anything* that might even tempt him to make a deal with me. The best I'll be able to do is insist that Robbie is right there, waiting for me, when I hand over the money."

Logan sat rubbing his jaw for a minute.

"What?" Ali finally said.

"I just don't like him calling all the shots. What if he has no intention of living up to his end of things? Even if you gave him the money, he could easily turn around and..."

Logan's words trailed off, but Ali didn't ask him to finish the sentence. She'd gotten the message loud and clear. Once she gave Bob the money, Robbie would no longer be safe. And neither would she. Swallowing hard, determined not to cry, she whispered, "So what do we do?"

He took her hands in his. "First, try not to be so upset. Wherever Robbie is, he's safe for the time being. And once you've talked to Bob, once you've explained that it's going to take five days to get the money, we'll have until Friday."

"Until Friday...to do what?"

"Well, I think we should try to figure out where Robbie is and get him back ourselves, before it comes down to having to hand over the money."

Ali sat fighting the sense that Logan was suggesting the impossible. There were millions of people in the city of Toronto. How could they hope to find one little boy? Especially when Wes Penna hadn't believed that even the police could manage it.

She didn't voice her doubts, though. She damn well wasn't going to give up before they'd begun, even if their odds on success were awfully low. And she wasn't going to let herself collapse into tears, either, even though not doing that was taking more willpower than she'd known she possessed.

"How do you think we should start?" she asked at last.

"Well, after you've talked to Robbie and Bob in the morning, and called that brokerage firm, I think we should pay Vinny Velarde a visit."

She shook her head in frustration. "If we talk to Vinny and Bob finds out...he said not to tell anyone I'd heard from him, remember?"

"Ali, I just don't think we'd be smart to do nothing. And if you're right about Vinny, if he's the only one who could be in on this with Bob, I'm sure he already knows you've heard from him."

"But if he *is* the one, he'd tell Bob everything I say and—"

"Maybe he would, and maybe he wouldn't. You don't know for sure how things stand between the two of them. And even if Bob *does* find out, there's not a lot he can do. As long as you've still got the money, he's not holding *all* the aces. And we have to keep the up-side in mind. Vinny probably knows where Bob is. Maybe even where Robbie is."

"Do you really think so?" The possibility gave her a tiny glimmer of optimism.

"I think, at minimum, he'll know how to get in touch with Bob, and that's a start."

"But how do we make him tell us?"

Logan hesitated, finally saying, "Let's sleep on that one. It's been a beast of a night, so let's just get some sleep and we'll talk about it in the morning."

"That's probably a good idea." Not that she expected to get even a minute's sleep, but at least they had the beginnings of a plan now, and that made things seem a little less impossible. Instead of lying awake worrying, she could spend the night thinking of a way to make Vinny tell them what he knew.

"Well, I guess I'll take Cody up to bed," Logan said. "You're going to be okay?"

She nodded again. "You go ahead. I'll turn off the lights down here."

Logan glanced over at his son, then back at her. "We're going to get Robbie home safely," he said quietly. "I promise we are." He leaned closer, brushed her cheek with a kiss, then murmured, "Night."

"Night," she whispered.

Watching him walk over to the love seat and pick up Cody made her throat ache. When Cody snuggled into his father's chest, she blinked back tears.

She was certain no one had carried Robbie to bed tonight. Certain no one had tucked him in. And as hard as she'd been trying not to dwell on how frightening this had to be for him, right now she couldn't think about anything else.

When Logan reached the doorway he looked back and smiled at her. She managed to keep her tears from escaping until he'd turned away again, but then they began to flow.

If only, long ago, she'd met a man like Logan, instead of Bob, this nightmare wouldn't be happening. If only Robbie had a father like Logan, instead of Bob, he'd be asleep in his own bed tonight.

Chapter Five

"Shh, everything's going to be all right," Ali murmured to Cody. He had the same scrubbed-fresh little-boy smell that Robbie had in the mornings, and it was enough to make her heart ache.

It was hardly Cody's fault, though, that he wasn't Robbie, so she cuddled him more closely on her lap. Her kitchen chairs might not have been designed for this sort of thing, but when he'd started crying halfway through his cornflakes they'd ended up here. He'd been in tears, off and on, for the entire hour he'd been up—despite Logan's attempt to paint an optimistic picture of Robbie being home soon.

"Daddy, what if the bad man comes back and takes me, too?" he asked between sobs.

"Cody, he's not going to do that," Logan said, pouring himself a glass of orange juice. "I promise he won't."

"But what if he does? What if he comes when you leave me at school and he takes me?"

Ali closed her eyes and tried to make her mind go blank, but she wasn't able to. When Cody was this upset at the *idea* of somebody taking him, how must

Robbie be feeling when somebody really *had* taken him? And what sort of scars would it leave?

She told herself not to think about that. It would only make this experience even more emotionally draining. The time to worry about long-term problems was after Robbie was safely home. Then they'd be able to deal with whatever the aftereffects were.

She looked over at Logan again. He was still trying to reassure Cody, but Cody wasn't buying it at all.

"Daddy, I don't want to go to school today," he whined. "I want to stay with you."

"Son, I'm afraid you can't. I..." He stopped speaking when Cody began crying again and buried his face against Ali.

Logan glanced across the table at her in obvious frustration.

She gave him a look that said she thought he should give in. She didn't know what they'd do with Cody when they went to see Vinny, but he was getting more and more upset, and he'd survive missing a day of grade one.

"Look, son," Logan said after a minute, "you can't stay with me because I'm not going to be home today. But how about this? What if, instead of school, I take you up to spend the day with Grandma and Grandpa? Would that be a good idea?"

Cody nodded without moving his face from Ali's shoulder.

"Okay, then you stop crying and I'll phone them right now." He glanced at his watch and frowned. "It's barely seven," he muttered to Ali. "Odds are, I'll wake them."

Absently thinking that Logan's parents couldn't be the early risers he and Cody were, she watched him dial. Then she half listened to his side of the conversation. The call, she gathered, *had* woken them. After he'd apologized to his mother for that he didn't say much, but he chose the words he did use carefully, letting her know there was a lot he was leaving out.

"Thanks a million," he finally told her. "I'll explain more when I get there."

He hung up and ruffled his son's hair. "Okay, let's go, sport. You run upstairs and wash your face again and we'll be on our way."

As Cody slid off Ali's lap, Logan glanced at his watch, saying, "I can easily make it back before nine."

She nodded, but his parents lived up in suburban Don Mills, and if the morning rush hour was bad...

He *had* to make it back before Robbie phoned, though, because she was really going to need his emotional support. How on earth was she going to reassure Robbie that everything would be fine when she was terrified it wouldn't? She was still worrying about that five minutes later, when Logan and Cody left. Once they were gone, she wandered aimlessly through the empty house, fighting to maintain what little control she still had over her emotions.

The oppressive silence didn't help. Normally, at this time on a Monday morning, Robbie would be noisily getting ready to leave for school—shouting to her about the boot or mitt that gremlins must have stolen during the night. Today, the house was as quiet as a tomb.

Tomb. She shook her head, knowing she was well on the way to worrying herself into a nervous breakdown. And she wasn't going to be any help to Robbie if she fell apart, so she couldn't let that happen. Somehow, she had to cope until he was safely home. She made a fresh pot of coffee, then poured herself some and sat down in the living room, pretending that she was actually relaxing.

Finally, at eight-twenty, she gave up the pretense and went over to the front window to watch for Logan. It was fully light outside now—a bright sun-shiny day that made the snow dazzle. Looking out at a morning like this would normally make her smile. Today, she knew *nothing* would make her smile. Not even Santa's sleigh, complete with every last reindeer, sitting on a lawn across the street.

Robbie had made a ritual of saying good morning to each of them through the window, and when she closed her eyes she could almost hear him rhyming off their names—saving Rudolph for last, because he liked him best. She swallowed over the lump in her throat and stared straight at the road, trying not to notice anything else.

When Logan hadn't appeared by eight-thirty she decided he'd gotten stuck in traffic. By eight-forty, she'd begun to visualize him inching his way down the Don Valley Parkway—commonly referred to by locals as the Don Valley parking lot. Then she looked back out and saw that he was actually pulling into her driveway. That caused her anxiety level to inch down a little. At least she was no longer alone.

Not wanting him to realize she'd just been standing waiting for him, she headed to the kitchen to fix him a coffee, putting it on the table just as he strode into the room.

"How's Cody?" she asked by way of greeting.

"He was fine by the time I left. My parents spoil him rotten, so he loves being with them. But what about you? You still hanging in okay?"

She nodded, glancing at what he was carrying—a screwdriver and a flat plastic thing the shape of a TV remote. It was three times larger, though, and had two long, plastic-coated wires protruding from one end and what looked like a telephone jack coming out of the other.

"My father's into electronic gadgets," he explained, setting it on the table. "Or battery-operated gadgets in this case."

"And this gadget is . . . ?"

"A special recorder for phone conversations. I'm just going to replace your answering machine with it until after we've taped the calls, okay?"

When she nodded again, he unplugged the jack on her machine.

"See all these playback controls?" he added, pointing to the row of dials. "You can do amazing things with what you tape—focus in on something and magnify it, enhance background sounds. It's way more sophisticated than we need, but I wanted to be able to replay the calls. If we're lucky, there'll be something useful on them."

"Like . . . ?"

"Who knows. Bob might let something slip. Or there could be background noise that would give us a clue. Even Robbie might say something that would help."

She watched as he moved the phone over to the table, then turned it upside down and started unscrewing screws. "This won't take long, will it?" she asked nervously. "It isn't that much before nine."

"I'll just be another minute." He pulled the bottom panel off the phone. "All I have to do is bridge this connection with the wires and we'll be able to plug the recorder in and out as easily as your machine... but what the hell is this?"

Ali stared at the exposed insides, seeing nothing that didn't look like she assumed it should. Logan, though, was removing a little silver thing. It reminded her of the tiny disk battery in her calculator.

"Son of a bitch," he muttered.

"What?"

He held the disk out in the palm of his hand. "This is a remote listening device. A transmitter. Somebody's had your phone bugged."

LOGAN HAD TURNED around the chair across the table from Ali's so he could straddle it, and they both sat watching the phone as the time drew closer and closer to nine.

Ali's gaze kept straying, though, to the little listening device that Logan had removed and left sitting on the table. She'd always thought phones were bugged by doing something with their wires in the basement or wherever, but that particular technology had apparently marched on without her knowledge. According to Logan, the little disk inside her phone was a transmitter that had enabled someone to listen in on her calls.

Or more likely, he'd said, to record them from a distance. That way, nobody had to spend time listening in. They could just check the tape every so often. The question was who, and the answer might well be Bob. And if it *had* been him, that shot to hell her theory that somebody must be in on this with him. He could have found out whatever he wanted to know just by taping her calls.

"It's nine o'clock," she finally murmured, checking her watch for at least the hundredth time that morning. "Bob told me *before* nine."

"Relax," Logan said. He reached across the table and squeezed her hand. "Just relax, it's going to ring any second."

He was right. It rang almost immediately—the sound momentarily paralyzing her.

Then Logan muttered, "Dammit," and she glanced at him.

Her gaze followed his back to the phone. The caller ID panel was flashing Unknown, just as it had last night, and she realized Logan had been holding out the same faint hope she had—that whoever Robbie was with wouldn't think to use a cell phone.

But he had, of course. Or, more likely, Bob had made a point of telling him to.

Heart pounding, hand trembling, she picked up the receiver.

"Mommy?" Robbie's thin little voice came across the line before she could say a word.

"Yes, darling, I'm here." She was flooded with relief at hearing him, but filled with anxiety by how frightened he sounded. Where was he? Who was he with? Was he all right?

Bob had told her no questions, but surely she could ask if he was all right.

"I'm okay," he told her when she did. "But, Mommy, they said I had to stay here a few days and I don't want to. Mommy..."

His voice broke, and hearing that almost broke her heart.

"Mommy...I watched all of 'Barney and Friends.' Right to the end. So I must be late for school already. So can you come get me right now?"

"Robbie, I'm going to come and get you just the minute I can. But it probably won't be today. You can phone me again tomorrow morning, though, and—"

He began to cry, and it was all she could do to hold back her own tears.

"Darling," she managed to continue, "listen to me. I want you to be a brave boy and try not to cry. More than anything in the world, I wish you could come home right now. But— Robbie, I know you don't understand what's happening, but I'll explain it all to you once you're here again. And I'll come and get you just as soon as I possibly can."

There was a tiny pause, then he sniffled and said, "I have to stop talking now, Mommy. But can't you *please* come get me today?"

"Oh, Lord," she whispered when a quiet click broke the connection. She hung up and buried her face in her hands, feeling as if the entire world was shattering around her.

"Ali?" Logan said. He'd come around the table and crouched beside her, resting his hand on her arm.

She gazed at him, her vision blurred.

"Just take a couple of deep breaths," he told her. "You're going to be okay."

"No...no, Logan, I had myself convinced I would be, but now I just don't think I am. I can't take this. Robbie thinks I've abandoned him and...it all hurts so much I really can't take it. And I'm not going to be able to talk to Bob when he phones. I want to kill him. I swear, if he was here right now I'd get a knife out of the drawer and try to kill him."

Logan reached past her and took the receiver off the hook once more. "There. Now he won't be able to get through until you're ready to deal with him."

"But I'll *never* be ready. Logan, you don't understand!"

"Shhhh," he whispered, drawing her up from the chair and wrapping his arms around her. "I *do* understand. I know how I'd be feeling if it was Cody. I know it's the worst thing you could ever have imagined happening, isn't it."

She nodded against him, her throat aching so hard she couldn't speak.

"I know...the worst possible thing. But it's happened, so we've got to deal with it. As much as I want to help you, you're the only one who can do some of it. For starters, you've got to be the one to talk to Bob.

So we'll just wait until you're ready before we put the phone back on the hook." He stopped speaking and just held her in his arms.

A moment later, one of Ma Bell's minions intruded, her mechanical voice filling the kitchen, saying, "Please hang up and try your call again...please hang up and try your call again."

They ignored the voice, but it was followed by a loud, insistent beeping that seemed to go on forever.

When that eventually ended, the only sound Ali could hear was the beating of Logan's heart. She rested her cheek against his chest and simply listened.

It felt incredibly comforting to have someone who cared hold her. The very hardest thing about trying to raise Robbie on her own was never having any emotional backup, never having a shoulder to cry on. But that was what Logan was giving her now—when she needed it more than she ever had before.

Gradually, listening to the reassuring rhythm of his heartbeat began to dilute the pain she was feeling. And the way he was holding her, his arms securely around her, made her start to think that maybe she *could* manage to talk to Bob.

Maybe, if she just stayed in Logan's embrace for a little longer, some of his strength would seep, osmosislike, from him to her.

LOGAN WANDERED from the fridge to the kitchen doorway and back, waiting for Bob Weyden's call and trying to keep his eyes off Ali. Each time he glanced at her, the memory of her body pressed against his flooded his mind. And that was damned disconcerting under the circumstances.

She was a friend in need, looking to him for comfort, and he was ... well, hell, every time he tried to comfort her he ended up struggling not to think of her as a desirable woman. Even with her face tearstained and her hair messy she looked so gorgeous that ...

Dammit. He'd been a complete idiot not to find out, long ago, whether there could be more than friendship between them. If so, things would have been entirely different by this point. And if not, at least he'd know where he stood. Looking over at her again, sitting quietly at the table, he started thinking about how great she'd been with Cody earlier.

He hadn't been exaggerating, last night, when he'd told her she was the best mother he knew. She was really good with kids. And with adults, too. She was quiet and thoughtful, yet she had a great sense of humor that made him always want to be around her.

So why had it taken him so long to click in on something so obvious? For almost an entire year he'd been telling himself he was only semi-interested in her, when all along he'd been falling in love with her.

He exhaled slowly, realizing it was the first time he'd actually admitted that to himself. Then the phone rang and his entire body tensed.

Leaning back against the counter, he did his best to hide his anxiety. When Ali's nod confirmed it was Bob, he gave her a thumbs-up for encouragement, then stood wishing he could hear what the guy was saying. He'd far rather be upstairs on the bedroom extension than down here, but he and Ali had decided he'd better not try that. Anyone listening carefully could always hear the click of a second line being picked up. And Bob would be listening carefully.

Besides, with the recorder, Logan would be able to hear every word later—as many times as he wanted. But he'd like to be hearing both sides of this conversation in real time.

Bob did most of the talking for the first minute; Ali barely uttered a word. But when she did start speaking she sounded surprisingly calm.

"I can't get it that fast," she said. "It's invested in mutual funds and it's going to take five days to free up.... Yes, I'm absolutely certain. I've already looked into it.... Bob, don't be ridiculous, where would stalling for time get me? You know how much I want Robbie back. Listen, I *swear* I'll get it for you. Don't you think you could let him come home now and... My word! That's what guarantee you'd have... Dammit, that's just not fair. I'd give you the money this minute if I could. But I just can't have it for you until Friday."

Logan watched her when she fell silent again.

After a few moments her face suddenly grew even paler and she said, "What?"

A second later she flashed him a distressed look. It made him wish even more that he was listening in.

"But last night you said I'd be *giving* you the money. I thought you meant I'd hand it to you and I'd get Robbie back right then and there.... I *am* cooperating, Bob. I'm giving you two million damned dollars! But I want my son in exchange for it, and this way..."

Logan could see she was fighting for control now and his heart began to pound. He had an almost overwhelming urge to grab the phone and threaten to tear Bob limb from limb.

"All right," Ali snapped. "All right, give it to me." She grabbed the pencil she had ready and started writing.

It took serious effort to stay where he was. He wanted to read what she was jotting down, but she sure didn't need him peering over her shoulder.

Ali glanced at Logan once more as she finished writing. He looked worried, but he gave her another thumbs-up.

She nodded and took a deep breath. She *had* to get through the rest of this conversation, because she still hadn't established the most important thing. "Fine," she managed to say. "I'll set things up this way. But exactly when do I get Robbie back?"

There was a fraction of a moment's silence, then Bob's voice came over the line again. "You'll get him as soon as I have confirmation the money's in my account. They've been told to fax me once it's been deposited."

She felt herself slipping into utter panic and clenched the receiver like a lifeline. "But... but what about the time difference? Europe is hours ahead of us. So what if my broker can't process this early enough on Friday? Or what if they don't fax you right away? What if they leave it until after the holidays? Bob, Sunday is Christmas Day. You just couldn't—"

"I'll do whatever I have to, Ali. So you'd better tell your broker to make sure things get done fast enough at both ends. Otherwise, Robbie won't be home for Christmas, will he?''

"All right," she replied. "All right, I'll do everything I can. And in the meantime, Robbie still phones me every day, right?"

"Sure. It's all arranged."

"And when will I hear from you again?"

"You won't. You know what to do, and I'll just have Robbie sent home once I know the money's been transferred. So stick around the house on Friday, eh? I wouldn't want him sitting outside in the cold."

"Dammit, Bob, if you don't send him home then, if you screw around with me, I'll—"

Logan stood waiting for Ali to go on but she didn't. Instead, she slammed down the receiver and looked over at him, saying, "He hung up on me. And Logan, the way he's got this set up..."

He could see she was almost in tears, but she waved her hand in the direction of the recorder, saying, "Play it back. Listen to what he told me to do. He's got things arranged so... oh, just listen to it."

Logan switched the recorder to Rewind, then to Play. The first bit on the tape was Robbie's call. Hearing both sides of the conversation brought a lump to his throat. He glanced across the table at Ali. She was listening with her fingers pressed to her lips, as if she could hold in her feelings that way. But when Robbie said, "Can't you *please* come get me today?" and the line went dead, tears began streaming down her cheeks.

Then the conversation with Bob began. When he started in on his instructions, Logan realized the guy hadn't missed a trick. He'd probably never even considered playing things straightforward, never even thought about a direct trade—Robbie for the money. And there was no way he'd be leaving any trail of what happened to that money once he had it. Ali's broker was to electronically transfer the funds into a numbered Swiss bank account.

That's what she must have been writing down, information on the account. And Swiss banks were so secretive even Interpol couldn't pry information out of them. He'd looked into that once, for a book.

"I'll do whatever I have to, Ali," Bob was saying on the tape. "So you'd better tell your broker to make sure things get done fast enough at both ends. Otherwise, Robbie won't be home for Christmas, will he?"

Logan clenched his fists. Never mind just tearing the guy limb from limb. That would be too damned good for him. Logan listened to the last bit of the conversation, then switched off the recorder. He hadn't picked up on any clue about where either Robbie or Bob were, but he'd play the tape again later and double-check.

At the moment, though, the last thing Ali needed was another run-through. He unplugged the recorder and plugged in her answering machine once more, giving her a little time.

When he finally looked over at her she said, "I'll call that brokerage firm in a minute or so."

"You're going to be okay?"

"Yes," she murmured, even though she looked anything but. "I just need a few minutes to... I just need a few minutes. And once I've phoned..."

She paused, her gaze flickering to the transmitter he'd removed from the phone. "Are we still going to visit Vinny?"

He hesitated and she said, "I thought of it, too, Logan. If *Bob* bugged my phone, maybe Vinny isn't involved after all. Maybe he doesn't know a darned thing."

"But maybe he does, so we've still got to talk to him. Ali, Bob might have had nothing to do with the bug. And even if he did, don't forget that Vinny—or the company, at least—got five million bucks because Bob played dead. Hell, from everything you've said, I still think Vinny's *got* to know what's going on. We should pick up your car before we go see him, though."

For a second, Ali didn't realize what Logan was talking about, then she remembered he'd driven her home in his Jeep last night—that they'd left her Probe in the clinic's parking lot.

Last night. How could that party have been only yesterday? It seemed forever since she'd seen Robbie. She blinked back fresh tears and concentrated on what Logan was telling her.

"We'll drive to Vinny's office separately," he was saying. "I'll leave ten minutes before you, park down on College and watch when you turn off Palmerston—just in case Bob has somebody tailing you. Then I'll follow you the rest of the way. If I hang back a few car lengths, and keep an eye out, we'll be sure we're on our own."

"And if we're not?" she asked uneasily.

"Then I'll pull up ahead of you. That'll be your signal to park and go into a store or something."

"Good thinking," she murmured. "But we've still got to figure out how to make Vinny talk."

"I had an idea about that. It involves your doing a good acting job, though." The way Logan eyed her as he said that, she could tell he wasn't sure she was up to it.

But she was. At least, she would be once she'd had time to pull herself together. "I'll do the best acting job you've ever seen," she assured him. "When I was talking to Bob... Logan, I'm even more certain now that we have to try to find Robbie ourselves. I got the feeling... I'm just not sure Bob has any intention of giving him back."

Chapter Six

Ali finished applying her makeup, then scrutinized the results and added more blusher. If Vinny realized how pale and drawn she actually was he'd know she was scared spitless. And she could hardly pull off an effective bluff if he knew that.

She *was* going to pull it off, though. After all, she was on a roll. Talking to Bob had undeniably upset her, but she'd made it through his call without completely disintegrating. And when she'd phoned the broker, she'd managed to sound so self-assured that she might have been giving him instructions about two hundred dollars, rather than two million.

So she'd be fine with Vinny, especially since Logan's plan was simplicity itself. They were just going to explain that Vinny had to tell them where both Bob and Robbie were. Otherwise, they'd call the police. They'd point out that if they did, Vinny would end up being charged as an accessory to a kidnapping, and also with defrauding the insurance company of five million dollars. If he was involved, even remotely, surely that would make him spill whatever he knew— as long as he was convinced she really *would* resort to calling the cops, when he undoubtedly knew Bob had told her it would be game over if she did.

But Vinny *would* be convinced, because she was going to put on an Academy Award-winning performance. She turned away from the dresser and checked her image in the cheval mirror. The tailored gray jacket, black pants and short, flat boots were perfect—serious, nonfrivolous clothes that said she meant business.

Reassured by that, she hurried out of the bedroom and down the stairs. By the time she and Logan had gotten back from picking up her car, the morning had been half-gone, and they wanted to arrive at Vinny's office well before noon. Not that they were *too* tight for time. Custom Cargoes was on Wellington, housed in one of the hundreds of ancient brick office buildings that sprawled to the west of Toronto's glass-and-steel financial center. As long as traffic wasn't bad, she could shoot down there in ten minutes or so.

Unless someone was following her, of course. She took her coat from the coat tree, reflecting on how many possibilities Logan had thought about that would never have occurred to her. It was probably because of his crime writing. But regardless of the reason, without him she'd have...

She'd have what? She considered that for a second, but she didn't have the slightest idea what she'd have done without him. He was as solid as a rock, and without his support she'd have been ready for a rubber room by now. If she'd fully realized what a great guy he was, right from the start...

She managed to force the *if* away, but seconds later an imaginary voice whispered, "Shoulda, woulda, coulda." It was too late, though, to think about what she should have done, or would have done, if she'd let herself get to know Logan better when they'd first met. The past was past. And, as for the future, until she got Robbie back her *present* was on hold, never mind her future. After that... well, after that Logan would be in L.A.

Before unlocking the door she gazed cautiously out to the street. Given the way things had been going, she wouldn't have been surprised to see an ominous-looking car with black windows parked in front of the house. But none of the parked cars seemed even slightly ominous. In fact, *nothing* seemed ominous. Sunlight was still dancing cheerfully on the snow. A pair of jays were calling raucously from the winter skeleton of the next-door neighbor's maple tree, and across the street Santa's reindeer were still poised to take to the sky. Everything seemed perfectly normal, so she clicked the dead bolt open and turned her attention to searching through her purse for her car keys—until she remembered she'd left them on the kitchen table.

Imagining Logan parked and waiting on College, wondering what on earth was keeping her, she hurried down the hall to retrieve them. When she walked back out of the kitchen there were two men standing on her front porch. They saw her the same instant she saw them.

For a moment she was frozen in place, like an animal caught in the glare of headlights—her throat sud-

denly dry and her palms wet, despite the fact that the
men were doing nothing menacing. They were simply
standing at her door in broad daylight. But she was
certain they hadn't come canvasing for Greenpeace or
anything like that. And even though they were both
wearing suits beneath their expensive-looking winter
coats, something about them said they weren't average, run-of-the-mill businessmen. In fact, something
about them said they were serious trouble.

Forcing herself to start walking toward the door, she
assessed them. The fortyish one was a little under six
feet tall and a few pounds overweight—a man she'd
pass on the street without noticing—except for the
long faded scar down his left cheek.

The younger one was in his late twenties and was
someone she definitely would notice. Bearded and
extremely large, he stood head and shoulders taller
than Scarface. As ridiculous as it was, he made her
think of Charles, the lowland gorilla who'd en-
tranced Robbie on their last visit to the zoo. Like
Charles, this *human* gorilla had a pushed-in nose and
beady brown eyes. He also had eyebrows that joined
together and an excessive amount of brown hair on his
head, as well as his face.

She reached the door, only too aware it was unlocked. So what should she do? Snap the dead bolt
into place right under their noses? An image of the
gorilla smashing a hairy fist through the glass made
her decide against that option.

"Mrs. Weyden," Scarface said, staring in at her.

It wasn't a question. He clearly knew who she was,
but she nodded an admission, anyway. Out of the

corner of her eye, she could see there was a car pulled up tightly behind hers in the driveway. A black Caddy with dark windows—precisely the ominous car she'd imagined seeing.

"A minute of your time," Scarface said.

That wasn't a question, either. In fact, it sounded as if he was delivering a line from a movie. Maybe he'd heard his favorite actor say it, thought it was cool and rehearsed it.

"I'm afraid you've just caught me on my way out," she started to explain. "I'm already late for—"

"We'll really only take a minute. Mrs. Weyden, we know you've talked to your husband. We know he has your son."

For half a second she wondered if these two could *possibly* be cops. Then she realized cops would have shown their ID. Whoever these guys were, though, maybe they'd come to offer their help. And regardless of the source, she'd consider any offer of help she got. Her stomach doing crazy flip-flops, she opened the door to the cold December air and ushered them into the hall.

"My name's Nick Sinclair, Mrs. Weyden," the older one said, introducing himself. "Nicky, if you like."

She didn't like, but she managed a polite smile.

"And this here's Chico Gonzalez." He gestured at the gorilla, who nodded to her.

"And you know where my son is?"

"Not exactly," Sinclair said.

"What do you mean, not exactly?"

"I mean it's like I said. We know your husband has him. But we don't know exactly where they are. We wanna find out, though...find your husband, I mean. It's not your son we're interested in."

The bitter taste of disappointment filling her mouth, she ruled out the possibility of unexpected help. "I don't know where my husband is," she told Sinclair. He was obviously the one in charge.

"No?" he said.

"No. Until last night, I didn't even know he was alive."

"Yeah, well, we always figured he was. And let's not play games, Mrs. Weyden. Maybe you don't know where he is right this minute, but you're gonna be seeing him when you give him the money."

Her mind racing, she tried to make sense of things, but there were too many blanks. To fill in at least one, she asked, "You know my husband?"

Sinclair shrugged. "We usta be business associates."

"Ah..." She didn't imagine, even for a second, that they'd been associated with the *legitimate* side of Bob's business. "Well, as I said, Mr. Sinclair, I don't know where my husband is."

"Yeah, well, like *I* said, you're gonna be seeing him when you give him the money."

But she wouldn't *be* giving Bob the money. Not face-to-face, at least. Nick Sinclair had some of his facts right and some wrong, and she didn't know what to make of that. Then she thought about the bug in her phone—and tried to remember exactly what had been said in each of her conversations with Bob.

Logan had removed that transmitter before Bob had called this morning, but it had been there last night. So if Scarface and the gorilla were the ones who'd planted it... "It was you who bugged my phone, wasn't it," she guessed.

Sinclair shrugged. "Like I told you, we always figured your husband was still alive. And that you'd hear from him. You or his partner."

"Vinny? You bugged Vinny's phone, too?"

"He have any other partners?"

She shook her head, not sure whether Sinclair was asking that as a serious question or just being sarcastic.

"Well, Vinny isn't the most cooperative guy. But you... well, we're counting on you to be more helpful. See, the point here is we got a little unfinished business with your husband, so we wanna talk to him. In person, like. And he said he'd be telling you about giving him the money this morning. So all I want you to do is tell me when and where you're gonna meet him."

Ali's throat felt so dry she doubted she could get words out. Last night, Wes Penna had suggested that Bob had been playing dead because he'd crossed the mob. But even if she hadn't had that possibility in the back of her mind, it wouldn't have been hard to guess what line of work Nick Sinclair and the gorilla were in. Or what their *unfinished* business was.

If anything happened to Bob, though, what would happen to Robbie? The way things stood, Bob was her only link to her son.

"Well?" Sinclair pressed. "When and where?"

She stared at him, utterly terrified and without the slightest idea what to say. Should she tell him the truth? That she wasn't going to be seeing Bob at all? Explain about his Swiss bank account?

But what if they didn't believe her? Then they'd probably try to beat the truth out of her. And if they *did* believe her... Lord, that might be even worse.

If they thought she'd be no further use to them ... she could suddenly visualize shoulder holsters with big guns hidden under those coats. Maybe, until she'd had time to think, the less she said the better.

"I don't know what the arrangements are going to be yet," she managed to say.

"Look, lady," Sinclair snapped, "don't hand me any bull. We heard what Bob said last night. He was going to give you the instructions this morning."

"But he didn't. I can't get the money right away, and when I explained that he just said he'd call me again."

"Dammit, lady, I'm losing my patience pretty quick here."

"No, I'm telling you the truth! Really. The money's tied up in mutual funds and it's going to take five days to— I can show you." The idea struck her with a flash of brilliance. "I can get the statement and show you if you want. It's just upstairs and it specifies the five days right on it."

"Okay," Sinclair said after a moment. "You go get it. Chico, go with her."

Ali turned and raced up the stairs. Above the hammering of her heart, she could hear Chico thudding after her. She grabbed the statement from the dresser, where she'd left it last night, and turned back to the bedroom door. Chico stepped silently aside to let her pass and she hurried down to the front hall again.

"It's right here on the back," she told Sinclair, frantically searching through the print to find the bit she needed. "Here . . . right here under Settlement Dates."

Sinclair followed the lines along with his finger as he read, then he turned the statement over and examined the front for a minute.

"Okay," he finally said, looking at her. "Okay, so when's he gonna phone again?"

"I don't know. Before Friday was all he said."

"That's the truth?"

She nodded fiercely, then did her best to hold his gaze so he'd believe her lie really *was* the truth.

"Okay, then I guess we gotta wait, eh? But me and Chico's gonna be keeping an eye on you while we wait. And when you get those instructions you're gonna tell us, right?"

She nodded even more fiercely.

"How about, when you got something you wanna tell us, you back your car into the driveway, instead of driving it in the way you usually do?"

The way she usually did. They'd not only bugged her phone, they'd *already* been keeping an eye on her. She tried to ignore the creepy-crawly feeling that knowledge produced and said, "Sure. Sure, I'll back it in."

"And you wouldn't even think of mentioning our little visit next time you talk to Bob, would you?"

"No. No, I wouldn't even think of it."

"Good. 'Cuz if he was to decide he didn't want to see us, 'cuz of something you said..." Sinclair reached out and touched her face, trailing his finger down her cheek, then under her chin.

His unmistakable message started her trembling.

"So we're real clear on that, eh? You won't be saying even a word."

"No. Not a word. But my son. This business you have with Bob..."

"Nobody's gonna hurt your kid, Mrs. Weyden. Not Chico or me, anyways." He jerked his head at Chico, then opened the door.

"You take care," he said, glancing back at her. "And don't forget, we're gonna be keeping an eye on you."

ALI BACKED OUT of her driveway, fear still making her hands shaky. A visit from guys like Sinclair and his friend wasn't something she could laugh off. Or simply put out of her mind, either.

They had no interest in harming Robbie, though. That was the important thing. "Nobody's gonna hurt your kid," Nick Sinclair had said, so she had that to cling to—assuming she could believe him.

But nobody *was* going to hurt Robbie, because she was going to get him back before Friday. And then Nick Sinclair...well, she had no idea what he'd do, but there were only so many things she could worry about at once.

She told herself to concentrate on her driving, and succeeded in making it down the block without wrapping her Probe around a pole. As she neared College, though, she thought about parking and finding Logan, rather than driving straight on to Custom Cargoes. He'd want to know about Sinclair and the silent Chico Gonzalez. And maybe, in however long it took to tell him, she could manage to stop trembling.

On the other hand, if she wasted any more time Vinny might go out for lunch before they got there. Glancing into the mirror again, she was glad to see there was still no sign of the black Caddy behind her. At least her new friends hadn't decided to keep *that* close an eye on her.

When she reached the stone pillars that stood on the corner of Palmerston—a pair of stately guards from the previous century—she gazed slowly along the row of parked cars on the far side of College. There was a streetcar partially blocking her view, and quite possibly hiding Logan's Cherokee. Or maybe he was farther along.

She was still undecided about parking and looking for him when, as if fate was telling her to carry on according to plan, one of the cars on College stopped and the driver gestured her into the intersection. With a quick wave of thanks she hung a left and started for Bathurst, keeping a close eye on the rearview mirror—glad her car was red, an easy color for Logan to spot.

Wherever he'd been parked, she should see him on her tail any minute. And, she thought uneasily, if she was observant enough she'd also see anyone else who might be following her. Just as she was turning south onto Bathurst a blue Jeep Cherokee came into view, half a dozen car lengths back—Logan behind the wheel.

The visible proof that he really was watching out for her, like a living guardian angel, made the remnants of her fear fade a little more. She only hoped he would stay back there, that he didn't signal her to stop because there was somebody else on her tail. She didn't want any more delays before they got to Vinny. Now that she knew it was Sinclair who'd bugged her phone, and not Bob, she was back to her initial theory.

Vinny had to have been in touch with Bob, feeding him information, helping him out. And whatever he knew about Bob's plans was going to bring her that much closer to finding her son. Maybe, as Logan had suggested earlier, Vinny even knew where Robbie was.

Telling herself not to let her hopes get *too* high, she spent the rest of the drive down to Wellington rehearsing what she'd say to that weasel Vinny. She found a parking space not far from Custom Cargoes, and while she was maneuvering her car over the icy ruts in it, Logan drove past. When he pulled into a space farther along, she headed down the block to meet him.

"What took you so long?" he demanded by way of a greeting. "I was sure I'd missed you somehow."

"Well, I had unexpected company." She turned back and started in the direction of Vinny's building with him. "Just listen to this."

LOGAN AND ALI PAUSED in the foyer of the old office building while she finished her story.

"So do you think I did the right thing?" she asked when she was done.

"I guess you must have. You're still in one piece." Logan forced a smile, trying not to let her see that he was scared to death for her. From Ali's descriptions, it seemed clear that the men were from the mob. The *mob,* for God's sake! Did she have any idea what they'd do if they found out she'd lied to them? Or *when* they found out, was more likely.

"I just didn't know what to tell them," she was going on. "I mean, they heard what Bob said last night—that I'd be *giving* him the money. And they made the same assumption I did, that he meant I'd be physically handing it over to him. So I was afraid to say that wasn't how it was going to be, afraid they'd think I was lying. And...oh, Logan, I was so frightened and I just didn't know."

He ran his fingers through his hair, resisting the urge to wrap his arms around her. He had to think, and holding her played havoc with his thought processes.

"I'm sure you did the best thing you could have," he said at last.

"Really?"

"Really. If you'd told them you wouldn't be seeing Bob...hell, I don't know what they'd have done. But this way they still think they're going to have a shot at getting their hands on him through you. That means you bought some time."

She looked so relieved he almost wished he hadn't reassured her. She might have done the best she could, but there was really nothing to be feeling relieved about. Just as Wes had suspected, Bob Weyden was running for his life. And now that the guys who wanted him dead were dragging Ali into their plans, there was only so much time she could buy. In the end... Logan couldn't stand even to speculate about that, so he asked if she was ready to face Vinny.

She gave him a wan smile. "After Nick Sinclair and Chico Gonzalez, facing Vinny's going to be a piece of cake."

He had another urge to wrap his arms around her, just because she was so gutsy. Instead, he followed her up the stairs and along the second floor hall to a door marked Custom Cargoes. Someone had decorated it with an evergreen wreath and a big red bow, but being reminded of Christmas did nothing to make him feel even a twinge of joy. He was too damned worried.

"Well, here goes," Ali murmured, opening the door.

He trailed along behind her, telling himself the smartest thing was to try to deal with only one issue at a time. And right now that meant not worrying about what the mob *might* do sometime in the future, and concentrating on learning what he could from Vinny Velarde.

The reception area contained a desk and file cabinets, along with typical waiting room furniture. Standing by the window was a receptionist in her early thirties—in the process of watering a potted Norfolk pine that had been hung with tiny ornamental balls and practically choked to death with silver garlands.

Logan decided she wasn't at all bad-looking, if a man's taste ran to leggy, top-heavy blondes with big hair, but she was decidedly unfriendly. There wasn't the slightest hint of Christmas spirit in the glare she shot them.

"Well, well," she muttered, her gaze settling on Ali. "Long time no see."

"Deloras," Ali said.

Logan glanced curiously at Ali, then back at the receptionist. Ali's tone was as frosty as Deloras's glare. Between the two, he could hardly keep from shivering.

"I want to talk to Vinny," Ali said.

Deloras shrugged. "You should have called. He's out of the office a lot, remember?"

Ali looked pointedly at the phone on Deloras's desk. Even though the receiver was on the hook, Logan noted, one of the line's lights was on.

"Are you saying he isn't in?" Ali said, her eyes still on the phone.

Deloras looked at it and shrugged again. "He's not seeing people today."

Without another word, Ali started across the reception area toward one of the two doors on the far wall. Logan followed along again, wondering what the story was with Deloras.

When Ali knocked on the office door, a male voice snapped, "What?"

"Vinny, it's Ali. I've got to talk to you."

Vinny muttered something Logan couldn't quite make out, but it sounded decidedly obscene. About a minute later, the office door opened.

"Oh, my Lord," Ali whispered, her hand flying to her mouth.

From her reaction, Logan concluded that Vinny didn't normally walk around with half-dried blood on his shirt, a face that resembled a piece of well-tenderized meat, and wearing a suit that looked like he'd worn it to go ten rounds with Mike Tyson.

"Come on in," he said, gesturing her inside as if Logan didn't exist.

When she didn't move, he looked at Logan. His eyes were so swollen it was impossible to tell what color they were, but the flesh around them was an unsightly red, beginning to turn purple.

Fleetingly, Logan wondered what he normally looked like. An average mid-forties guy, he decided. Average height and weight, with graying brown hair combed forward to hide a receding hairline.

"He's a friend, Vinny," Ali was explaining, taking Logan's arm and drawing him into the office with her. "Logan Reed."

Logan extended his hand, although he wasn't sure normal etiquette was appropriate with someone who'd obviously had the crap beaten out of him not long ago.

Vinny didn't shake, so he decided it must not be.

"Put the answering machine on and go for lunch," Vinny told Deloras. "Right now. And bring me back a pastrami on rye, okay?"

She shrugged. "Sure. Nice seeing you again, Ali," she added sarcastically as Vinny shoved his door closed.

"Vinny, what happened?" Ali asked. "You look like—"

"I looked a hell of a lot worse before I got cleaned up." Vinny limped over to his desk and slumped into his chair. "Take off your stuff and have a seat."

"Shouldn't you go to a hospital?" Ali asked once she and Logan were sitting in the visitors' chairs.

"No, it looks worse than it is. Nothing's broken."

"But when Mimi sees you..." Ali paused, turning and explaining to Logan that Mimi was Vinny's wife.

"Fortunately," Vinny muttered, "she's out of town. Gone to a spa to rest up before Christmas.

"Go figure women, eh?" he added, glancing at Logan through the narrow slits beneath his swollen eyelids. "She's resting up for the *holidays*."

"But what happened to *you?*" Ali asked a second time.

"When I tell you, you're not going to believe it." Vinny looked in Logan's direction again—pointedly, this time.

"You can talk in front of him," Ali said.

"You sure?"

"I'm sure."

"It's about Bob."

"Good. That's who we came about."

Ali leaned forward in her chair to listen; Logan got a little more comfortable in his. He had a feeling they were going to be in Vinny's office for a while, but at least they were getting on topic now.

"When I came in this morning," Vinny began, "there were a couple of guys waiting for me. They—"

The sound of a muffled sneeze, directly outside the door, stopped him mid-sentence. The sneeze was immediately followed by a knock.

"What?" Vinny called.

The door opened and Deloras stuck her head into the office. "You want *hot* mustard on that sandwich or not?"

"What kinda question's that? Don't I always want hot mustard?"

She shrugged. "I just figured maybe you wouldn't today. I mean, I figured maybe you wouldn't feel like spicy with all those bruises, because...oh, never mind. I was just trying to be thoughtful."

Vinny waited until she'd closed the door again, then said, "So where was I?"

"There were a couple of guys waiting for you," Logan reminded him.

"Oh, yeah. So they wanted to know where Bob was, and when I told them he was six feet under, somewhere in Nicaragua, they didn't buy it—just kept going on about how they knew he wasn't really dead and trying to make me tell them where he was."

"Oh, Lord," Ali whispered. "That's what he meant."

"Who meant what?" Vinny said.

"I...let me try to remember his exact words. Something about your not being cooperative. But I didn't realize...the two guys who did this, their names were Nick Sinclair and Chico Gonzalez?"

"Yeah. How did you know that?"

"Because they came to see me, too. After they'd seen you. I mean, I didn't realize they'd already been to see you...that they'd done anything like this. But when you didn't tell them, they tried me."

"Tell them what?" Vinny demanded.

"Where Bob is."

Vinny slowly leaned forward in his chair and stared across his desk at Ali. "What the hell," he finally asked, "is going on here?"

"They weren't just fishing," she said evenly. "They *know* Bob's alive. And I gather they want to change that."

"Ali... you didn't actually buy their routine, did you? *You* know Bob's dead. So do I. So what the—"

"Vinny, dead men don't phone their wives and snatch their sons, so drop the act, okay? We *all* know he's very much alive, and right here in town."

Logan thought Vinny went white at that, but his face was so bruised it was hard to be sure.

"You're serious," he said after a moment.

"You're damned right, I'm serious. And I want to know where Bob's got Robbie. Right now."

"You said he phoned you? You're *sure* it was Bob?"

"Vinny, don't do this to me. I know you helped him get Robbie and—"

"That bastard," Vinny hissed. "I should have *known* he wasn't really dead. It was too good to be true."

Chapter Seven

Walking in to discover Vinny looking as if he belonged in an emergency room had really thrown Ali a curve. And his apparent shock at the news that Bob was alive had given her second thoughts about the original plan of attack.

So instead of immediately threatening to call the police and implicate Vinny in kidnapping and fraud, she'd proceeded more slowly, waiting to see what he had to say and saying as little as possible herself. What you saw wasn't always what you got with Vinny, so she certainly hadn't bought right into his know-nothing routine. And she hadn't entirely ruled out the possibility that everything she said would be repeated to Bob—which meant the less she said the better.

But when Vinny insisted that the first he'd heard of anyone thinking Bob was alive had been when Nick Sinclair came calling, Ali gritted her teeth and played along—outlining the basic details of the kidnapping and of her subsequent conversations with Bob. Finally, when she not-too-subtly pointed out that Vinny was the most obvious person to be helping Bob, he started talking.

All he did, though, was swear up and down he'd been *certain* Bob was dead and buried in Nicaragua, and that he couldn't believe Ali thought he might be party to something that would hurt either her or Robbie.

After he'd gone on that way for ten minutes non-stop, she was so upset she was having trouble thinking straight. If Vinny was lying, he was doing one hell of a convincing job. And if he was telling the truth, he knew nothing that would help her find Robbie.

She just prayed he was lying, and that they'd finally get the real story out of him. Because if Vinny wasn't Bob's accomplice, she had no idea who was.

"Can I interrupt here for a minute," Logan said at last. "It would be a lot easier to believe you weren't involved if we had some proof."

"Yeah? What kind of proof?"

Logan turned to Ali. "Tell Vinny what Sinclair said about bugging his phone."

"What?" Vinny yelped. "My phone? You mean this phone here?"

She shrugged uncertainly. "From what he said, I wasn't *sure* whether he had or not. But he bugged mine, so—"

"He admitted that?"

"Well, Logan had already found the bug, so it wasn't a big secret. But that's how Sinclair knew Bob had called me. And he said he'd been sure Bob would get in touch with either you or me, so I assumed..." She paused, because Vinny had stopped looking at her and was eyeing his phone.

"Want me to check it?" Logan asked him.

"Yeah, be my guest."

"I need something to get the screws out."

"I think there's a screwdriver here someplace." Vinny shoved himself up, limped over to a cabinet next to the door and began rummaging around.

"If his phone's bugged, too," Ali whispered, leaning closer to Logan, "does that means he's telling us the truth?"

"It makes it more likely," Logan whispered back.

"It's not here," Vinny muttered. "Maybe Deloras was using it," he added, reaching for the door handle.

When he opened the door, Deloras Gayle was standing directly outside. Even if her face hadn't gone red, Ali would have been positive that she'd had her ear to the door.

"What are you doing back already?" Vinny demanded.

"I brought your sandwich. It's on my desk," she added when he looked pointedly at her empty hands. "I was just coming to ask if you wanted me to make coffee."

"No. No, thanks. But I'm looking for the screwdriver. You got it?"

"I think it might be in my desk."

"What's the story with her?" Logan murmured as Vinny followed her across the reception area. "She just naturally nosy or what?"

"Probably." Ali said. "But mainly, I think that when she just *happened* to be standing outside the door the first time—when she supposedly came to ask

Vinny about the mustard—she overheard enough to know we were talking about Bob. And . . . well, that would have made her really curious."

"Oh?"

Ali shrugged. She'd already told Logan so many embarrassing details about her marriage, what did one more matter?

"Deloras was what you might call the final straw that broke Bob and I up," she explained. "Not that I'd have stayed with him much longer, anyway, but when I found out he had something going with her, it sped things along."

"He was married to *you* and fooling around with *her?* That's tough to believe."

"Thanks. But if you'd known Bob . . . He was constantly proving things to himself, and I guess having an affair made him feel like more of a man. After I'd caught on, he swore she'd never really meant anything to him. And that might have been true."

"Oh?" Logan prompted when she didn't elaborate.

"Well . . . she called me once, to try and convince me not to give Bob such a hard time about getting a divorce. When I said he'd never even asked for one, she went off like a rocket. I was never sure if it was because she *didn't* believe me or because she *did.* I think he was using me as an excuse because he didn't want to get permanently tied up with her."

"She sounds like quite the character—all around," Logan said quietly, nodding toward the open door.

From beyond it, they could hear Deloras snapping at Vinny about something.

Ali shrugged. "They've always *sounded* as if they've got no use for each other, but that's just the way they relate. Actually, Vinny thinks she's great at her job. At least, I remember he always used to."

"And what does she think about Vinny?"

"Who knows?" Ali lapsed into silence and sat listening while Vinny and Deloras snarled away at each other in the reception area.

"THIS DO?" Vinny asked, finally reappearing with a steel letter opener and shoving his door closed again. "We can't find the screwdriver."

Logan nodded. It had a thin, flat-ended handle, so it would probably work. He started unscrewing the phone's bottom plate while Vinny slumped down behind his desk once more.

Inside the phone was the same sort of little transmitter that had been in Ali's.

"Son of a bitch," Vinny muttered when he saw it.

Ali sat staring at it, and Logan could tell her sense of frustration was growing stronger yet. She'd been totally convinced Vinny had been in on the kidnapping. But it was looking more and more as if she'd been wrong. Of course, things weren't always the way they seemed.

"Dammit, Ali," Vinny was saying, "is that bug enough proof for you? If I *had* been talking to Bob, don't you think Sinclair and his muscle would have been around to see me before today? And if I knew *anything,* don't you think I'd have told them the minute they showed up? Do you think I'd let Sinclair's pet ape practically kill me because I wanted to protect Bob?''

"I don't know what I think! Vinny, for all I know, you and Bob cooked up the entire story about his death to collect on the insurance. For all I know, you split that five million with him and—"

"You don't know what you're talking about. You have no idea what was going on before Bob disappeared. You never had a clue what he was doing when you were living with him, let alone after you split. If he's really still alive, then that whole deal in Nicaragua was his way of trying to bail out. I sure wouldn't have helped him, though."

"No? Not even when it was worth five million to you? Vinny, *you're* the one who collected on that policy. *You're*—"

"Don't I wish! Don't I just wish I'd really gotten something out of it. But that money was gone the day I got the insurance check. Every cent of it, thanks to Bob."

"Gone where?" Logan asked.

"To somebody Bob owed, that's where. Somebody who figured his partner should make good for him and was leaning on me damned hard."

Vinny turned his swollen face toward Ali again. "Why do you think I was so frantic when the insurance company was stalling? Why do you think I went all the way to Nicaragua to see what I could find out? Because Bob left me holding the bag, that's why."

While Vinny was talking, Logan's mind was working at top speed. Whenever he got hung up with a plot, couldn't figure out where a book should go next, he tried to consider any and all possible directions. And it sounded like Vinny had a direction worth considering.

"Bob left you holding what bag?" he asked.

"That's none of your business," Vinny snapped.

"Well, I'm not so sure it isn't. At the moment, my business is trying to help Ali find Robbie. And if we can figure out who *did* know Bob was really alive, who helped him with the kidnapping, it could be the key. So why don't you tell us about the trouble he was in before he disappeared? There might be something that would give us a clue."

"No, nothing I know would help."

"Vinny," Ali murmured, "Robbie's gone. How can you not at least try to help me?"

Vinny started to rub his jaw, then winced and lowered his hand. "What about the insurance company?" he asked her after a minute. "Are you going to tell them Bob's not really dead?"

"I...I don't know. I mean, I know that legally I have to, but if I give the two million to Bob..."

"Then you won't be able to pay them back. You'll be up the same creek as me. So you see why I'm asking? We're in the same boat, only I'm in for five million, not two. So, if I try to help you, are you going to help me?"

"You mean not tell them Bob's alive."

"Yeah, that's exactly what I mean."

"Vinny, I just haven't been able to think that far ahead. All I can think about right now is Robbie."

"Yeah...yeah, of course. And I feel real bad for you. You know I do. But if that insurance company comes asking for its money back, I'll have serious problems. Hell, at the very least they'll bankrupt me. And if they decide to try convincing some judge that I was in on Bob's scheme, I could end up in jail. But if you don't say anything, we'll both be home free."

When Ali glanced anxiously at Logan, he knew exactly what she was thinking. Earlier, on their way to pick up her car, they'd discussed the big picture. She knew that both she and Vinny were going to have to pay back the money—regardless of what she said or didn't say.

Sooner or later, if nobody else spoke up, Kent Schiraldi was bound to. He knew the insurance company had paid Ali the two million because Bob was supposed to be dead. But Kent had been right there in Nancy's office the first time Bob had called. And, as Ali had told Vinny, dead men didn't phone their wives and snatch their sons.

So, with Kent knowing that the insurance company had been defrauded, he was skating on thin professional ice by keeping quiet about it for even a few days. If Ali hadn't begged him and Nancy not to say anything until Robbie was safe, he'd probably have blown the whistle already.

"Well?" Vinny pressed. "Have we got a deal, Ali?"

"Look," Logan said before she could answer. "We just can't know how everything's going to play out. But I'll promise you this much, and I think Ali will, too. You cooperate with us now, tell us about that trouble Bob was in before he disappeared, and if the insurance company *does* hit you with fraud charges we'll back you up—testify we're certain you didn't intentionally defraud them, that you honestly believed Bob was dead, the same as Ali did.''

Vinny stared at the carpet for a long minute. "That's something, I guess," he finally muttered. "But I can't tell you much. If you end up getting asked any questions, the less you know the better.''

Logan wasn't sure whether Vinny was worried about them being questioned by the insurance company, the police or Nick Sinclair. It also wasn't clear *who* would be better off if they didn't know too much. But he just nodded for Vinny to go on.

"Well, this morning wasn't the first time I'd met Sinclair," he began. "He was the guy Bob owed, the one leaning on me for the money. Not long after the finger came in the mail . . .'' He paused and glanced at Ali.

"I told Logan about that," she said.

"Okay, so I'd gotten the finger—with the note saying double-dealers don't live long in Nicaragua. Then the police had identified the finger as Bob's and . . . well, once they'd done that it seemed obvious to everyone that he was dead. To everyone except the insurance investigator, that is. Then, a couple of weeks later, Sinclair and his muscle showed up.''

"And *that* was the first time you met them?" Logan asked.

"Yeah. Sinclair had heard Bob was dead, so he came to explain to me that Custom Cargoes owed him money. *Mega*-money. Suddenly, with Bob out of the picture, he'd decided it was the company that owed him, not Bob, personally. And—''

"Wait a sec," Logan interrupted. "You said he came to *explain.* So you didn't even know Bob owed anybody money until then?"

"I didn't know anything about *anything* until then. Nothing. Not that Bob had been playing games. Not that he'd been in trouble before he went to Nicaragua. Nothing. But it turned out he'd been handling shipments for Sinclair—off the books, of course, or I'd have been clued in. And as I said, with Bob out of the picture, Sinclair decided I should pay what he figured was owed him."

"Which was this mega-money."

Vinny nodded. "See, Custom Cargoes is always trucking stuff across the border. That's what import-export is all about, eh? And according to Sinclair, Bob had a lot of the bigger rigs hauling...well, stuff that wasn't exactly what their paperwork specified."

"Stuff?" Logan said.

"Ah...this gets into the part where the less you know the better."

When Logan simply waited, Vinny shrugged, saying, "Sinclair's got his hand in the underground market. Booze, tobacco, *stuff.* You know. But that's something I'll deny saying if this conversation ever comes back to haunt me."

Logan glanced at Ali. She'd mentioned suspecting Bob of running illegal booze, but even if she hadn't he'd buy Vinny's story—the main facts, at least.

He doubted it was *entirely* accurate, especially the bit about Vinny knowing nothing. There was only so much Bob could have done, even off the books, before Vinny would have gotten wise. But the basics weren't hard to believe. Smuggling illegal liquor into the country was big business. And if you were smuggling one thing, why not a whole variety?

"At any rate," Vinny was going on, "Sinclair said he'd discovered Bob was shorting the shipments."

"Which means what, exactly?" Ali asked.

"Which means, exactly, that Sinclair was paying for more product than was getting to his customers."

"But wouldn't he have caught on to that right away?"

"Obviously he didn't."

Ali eyed Vinny doubtfully. "Nick Sinclair didn't strike me as a dummy."

"No, but there are ways of shorting that are hard to pick up on. And when people are buying from the mob, it takes a lot to make them complain. So by the time Sinclair caught on, Bob was into him for big, big bucks. And that's when Bob decided to go check out his business prospect in Nicaragua."

"Because Sinclair wanted his money back and Bob didn't have it," Ali concluded. "But five million dollars? You said you handed over every cent of the insurance money, so you're saying Bob cheated the mob out of *five million dollars?*"

"Actually, according to Sinclair it was more than that. But we settled on five because it was what the policy was worth. The way he looked at things, he was giving me a break—not making me sell the company to come up with the rest."

"He's a real prince," Logan muttered.

"And that's why he wants Bob dead?" Ali asked. "Because he didn't get all his money back? That *is* why he wants to find Bob, isn't it? To kill him?"

"Yeah," Vinny said, "but it's not really because of the money anymore. It's just a matter of principle now. Guys like Sinclair don't take kindly to being cheated. Or lied to. Which is more stuff I'd never admit saying."

Logan looked anxiously at Ali. Her eyes were wide with fear, and she was clearly wondering the same thing he was. How unkindly would Sinclair take it if he learned *she'd* lied to him?

LOGAN FOLLOWED ALI back from the restaurant and pulled into her driveway behind her. He'd suggested grabbing a late lunch while they were out, but it had been a bad idea. Neither of them had felt like eating. All they'd done was talk in circles about the hour they'd spent with Vinny.

The bottom line, of course, was that it hadn't gotten them anywhere. Vinny knew nothing—unless he'd been putting on a great performance. And that was a possibility they had to keep in mind, even if it seemed a remote one. After all, he'd taken quite a beating. On the other hand, wouldn't most guys take a beating if the stakes were five million bucks?

For all they knew, Vinny might even have some deal going with Sinclair. Then, both the beating and that bug in his phone would have been only for show. No, they hadn't learned a damned thing for sure. Climbing out of his Jeep, Logan silently trailed Ali into the house.

"I'll make some coffee," she murmured, hanging up her coat.

He nodded, tossed his jacket on the coat tree, then followed her down the hall.

When she reached the kitchen doorway her body tensed. Over her shoulder, he could see the message light was flashing on her machine.

She hurried across and pushed the playback button. The first message was from Nancy McGuire, saying she hoped Ali was holding up all right and asking her to call back with news on what was happening. The second was from a woman who identified herself as Celeste and wanted to know what time Ali would like her to come for Christmas dinner.

"Who's Celeste?" he asked as the woman began a story about a shopping trip to the Eaton Centre.

"Bob's mother," Ali said.

That took him by surprise and it must have showed, because Ali launched into an explanation.

"She's a sweet lady. She just happened to have a rotten son, and I just happened to marry him. But Robbie's her only grandchild so...well, it never seemed right to cut her off just because of Bob. And she has no other family to be with on Christmas Day, so I thought...but, oh, Lord, Logan, what do I do now? Tell her what's happening? Tell her that Bob really isn't dead? She'd be frantic with worry about Robbie, but..."

"Let's talk about it later," Logan said as Celeste finished the story about her shopping and the machine beeped to its final message.

It was a combined one from his mother and Cody, wanting to know what time Logan was coming to pick Cody up, and inviting him to have dinner there.

When Cody ended with a, "Bye, Daddy, bye, Ms. Weyden," Ali pushed Rewind and glanced at Logan, disappointment written across her face. "When I saw the message light flashing I thought maybe...silly, eh? I know I won't hear from Robbie again until the morning."

She turned back to the counter and busied herself with the coffee, while Logan stood trying to decide when he *was* going to pick Cody up. The idea of Nick Sinclair and Chico Gonzalez *keeping an eye* on Ali was enough to make his blood run cold, yet there wasn't a damned thing he could do about it. What he *could* do, though, was make sure Cody wasn't within ten miles of the neighborhood while those characters were hanging around.

He knew worrying along that line wasn't rational. There was no reason for them to have the slightest interest in Cody. Even so, he'd feel better knowing someone was watching his son every minute, and he couldn't be doing that and helping Ali at the same time.

So, all in all, the smartest thing would be to have his parents keep Cody for a while longer. But how would Cody feel about not coming home and getting back into his normal routine? Logan watched Ali pour the coffee, wishing he'd been taking some of her psychology courses with her.

"Let's sit in the living room," she suggested, handing him one of the mugs. "In here, I can't seem to keep my eyes off the phone."

He followed her down the hall again and sank onto the couch beside her, asking, "What do you think I should do about Cody? You figure he'd be upset if I suggested leaving him at my folks for another day or two or... Ali?" he murmured, realizing tears were streaming down her face. "Ali?" Taking her coffee, he set both mugs on the end table, then turned back to her.

When Logan put his arm around her shoulder, Ali curled into him, pressing her face against his chest. She almost never cried, but since yesterday she'd felt within seconds of tears every single minute.

His holding her helped, though. His touch reminded her she wasn't facing this alone, and the strong warmth of his body felt reassuring against hers. She took a few deep breaths, trying her hardest to regain control.

"What?" he murmured against her hair. "What? Is it that we didn't learn anything from Vinny?"

"Partly. And partly...oh, Logan, when Cody asked about coming home, you can just decide when... but this morning, when Robbie asked me that...he wanted me to come and get him right then, but I couldn't and...and what if he never comes home? What if..." Her tears won out again, and she buried her face more tightly into Logan's sweater.

"Don't," he whispered. "Don't do this to yourself. We'll get him back."

"Will we?" she managed to say, looking at him once more. "How? Tell me how, because right now I just can't make myself believe we really will."

He wiped away her tears, then gently kissed her forehead, murmuring, "You can't make yourself believe it right now because you're too wound up to think straight. That's all it is. So we're going to take a little time out. We're not going to talk about it any more for a while. Okay?" When she nodded, he kissed her forehead again. "Good. Then, later, we'll come back at it fresh. Figure out where to go from here. We're a good team, Ali. And we're going to make everything turn out fine."

She bit her bottom lip, determined not to cry anymore. But if she tried to say even one word...

Logan rested his fingers beneath her chin, tilting her face up a little, and she gazed at him, her eyes swimming with the tears she was holding back.

"Oh, Ali," he murmured, "I'd give anything to make it better for you right this minute."

"You are," she whispered. "You are making it better. Logan, if it wasn't for you I don't know what I'd do."

He held her gaze for a moment longer, then leaned closer and kissed her.

She wrapped her arms around his neck and melted against him. His lips were warm and firm against hers, and his kiss made her feel as if, just possibly, he was right. They *were* a good team. So maybe, between the two of them, they *would* make everything turn out fine.

"What?" she asked when he stopped kissing her.

"I . . . look," he murmured, his breath fanning her mouth with warmth, "I guess I couldn't have picked a worse time to do that, could I? I'm sorry if—"

"Don't be. You couldn't have picked a *better* time. It feels good to be held, Logan. I don't feel so afraid in your arms . . . or so helpless. Your timing was perfect . . . and so was what you were doing." She tangled her fingers in his hair and drew his lips back to hers.

Chapter Eight

Ali shrugged into her coat and walked Logan out to the driveway, unable to stop at the front door and say goodbye. Something had clearly gone haywire with her self-control, so when they reached his Jeep she shoved her hands into her pockets to keep from touching him.

Impossible as it seemed, when the situation with Robbie already had her in a state of emotional overload, kissing Logan had released a brand-new flood of emotions. The smoldering attraction she'd developed for him had suddenly burst into flames. And its happening *now* had taken her completely by surprise.

"You won't change your mind?" he asked, bringing her back to the moment. "My mother's a great cook, and getting away from here for a few hours would do you good."

"No. Thank her for inviting me, but I'd rather be home. Just in case."

"Well, you never know. Robbie's a resourceful little guy."

She pushed her hands even more deeply into her pockets. Logan's thoughts were so closely in tune with hers it was eerie. She could talk in half sentences and he still knew what she meant, even when she was thinking about crazy things like Robbie getting away from whoever had him and trying to reach her.

"You're sure you'll be okay, though?" Logan murmured, resting his hand against her cheek.

Its reassuring warmth made her wish even more that he didn't have to go.

"I really hate to leave you here alone," he was saying. "Maybe I should phone them back and—"

"No, you can't explain things to Cody over the phone. You've got to be sure he understands."

"Yeah...yeah, you're right." Logan glanced down the street to his own house. "I don't really need to take any of his things. My mother keeps some basics up there. But maybe I'd better feed Sammy before I go. It'll only—"

"No, just get going. The traffic will already be heavy, so I'll feed him."

"Sure you don't mind?"

"Mind?" If her sense of humor had been functioning the questions would have made her laugh out loud. "After all you've been doing for me, you think I'd mind feeding your cat?"

He grinned. "Actually, I was thinking how evil-tempered he can be—especially when you try to pawn off dry food on him. But there's a half full can of the good stuff in the fridge someplace. So...you want me to stop by when I get home? Just check in with you?"

"If my lights are on. I didn't sleep last night, so I'm not going to stay up late."

"Well, if I don't see you tonight, I'll come over first thing in the morning. And as soon as you've heard from Robbie, we'll decide on our next move."

Logan leaned closer and brushed her lips with a gentle kiss. Then he slid into the driver's seat, slammed the door and backed out onto the street.

She stood watching the Cherokee until it disappeared, thinking that her timing had gone every bit as haywire as her self-control. What had happened with Logan . . . well, what had happened was that her hormones had ganged up on her while she'd been too busy worrying to notice. And her brain had been too preoccupied to remind her that he'd be gone in a few weeks.

Instead of watching his car heading for Don Mills, she'd be watching his plane take off for Los Angeles. So, after all the time she'd gone along denying she felt anything but friendship for him, why on earth had she let this happen now? Starting for his house, she told herself she hadn't *let* it happen. It just had. And she didn't regret it. Being in his arms had given her more comfort than she could have hoped for.

From here on in, though, she had to remember things were about to come to an abrupt end between them. And only a fool would get in any deeper with a man who already had one foot out the door. As her mother had always said, "Never start something if you know you won't be able to finish it."

Her mother, she reflected, turning into Logan's yard, had been a smart lady. When she glanced at the house, she spotted Sammy's little gray face in the living room window. He was peering eagerly at her from his perch on the back of the couch, so she dug her keys out of her pocket and hurried up the steps. Since she'd moved here, she and Logan had done almost all of each other's baby-sitting. So they'd long ago exchanged house keys and...

The thoughts flowing from that one brought a lump to her throat. She'd give anything in the world to open the door and hear Robbie and Cody demanding cookies and whooping with laughter. But the only sound that greeted her was Sammy's wailing. He'd scurried into the front hall and was already three heartrending yowls into his dying-of-starvation monologue.

Logan described him as a highly verbal cat, but she suspected that if they could translate those yowls into English they'd discover he was actually just a whiner. She followed him into the kitchen, found the opened can of food and spooned what was left into his bowl. Then, just as she was rinsing the can for the recycling box, there was a knock at the front door.

Her heart anxiously skipped a beat. This morning, her unexpected visitors had been bad, bad news. Reminding herself she was in Logan's house, that whoever had knocked was *his* visitor, she headed into the hall.

Like her own front door, the top half of Logan's was glass. Standing on the other side of it was a woman—about thirty, extremely attractive, perfectly made up, and dressed to kill in a fitted burgundy suede coat. When she saw Ali, a puzzled look flickered across her face. Then she smiled.

"Yes?" Ali opened the door a few inches.

"Is Logan home?"

"No, I'm afraid he's not."

"Cody, then? Are you baby-sitting?"

Ali shook her head. "No, I'm sorry, there's no one in right now."

"Oh? Then who are you?" The woman's tone had suddenly become less friendly, almost making Ali wish she hadn't answered the door.

"I'm a neighbor," she offered.

"Oh, is that all." The smile reappeared. "Well, are they going to be long? Maybe I should come in and wait."

"No, it would be a long wait. Logan only left a few minutes ago and he won't be back until after dinner, so—"

"Rats! I guess I should have called ahead, but I wanted to surprise them. I'll just come in long enough to phone for a taxi, then. I let mine go."

The woman pushed the door open farther and walked in past Ali, exclaiming, "Lord, he's still got that obnoxious cat! I don't believe it. Sammy, any normal man would have drowned you by now."

Ali glanced back along the hall. Sammy was standing outside the kitchen doorway watching them. His yellow eyes were narrowed and he was holding his tail straight up and swishing it back and forth. According to Logan, that indicated anger, so the momentary surge of affection she felt for the cat made no sense.

She turned curiously back to the woman. "I'm sorry, but I don't know who you are—to tell Logan."

"Oh, I'm Loretta."

"Loretta?"

"Yes . . . Loretta Carlisle . . . Logan's wife."

LOGAN'S MOTHER GAVE HIM a farewell kiss, then disappeared to load the dishwasher. Cody, though, wasn't quite ready to see his father leave.

"And you'll phone me in the morning," he said, wrapping his arms even more tightly around Logan's neck.

"I promise."

"And I won't get in trouble 'cuz I'm not at school."

"No, I'll call your teacher and explain."

"And Robbie's gonna be home soon."

"I promise," Logan said again. It was a promise he intended to do everything in his power to keep, but what would happen if . . . ?

He tried to force his mind from that question.

"Before Christmas *for sure*," Cody said.

"Absolutely."

"And me, too. I'll just be staying with Grandma and Grandpa another day or two."

"I thought you liked it here," Logan's father said, holding out his arms to take Cody.

Logan breathed a sigh of relief. He'd been starting to have visions of still being trapped in his parents' front hall come midnight.

"I *do* like it here," Cody assured his grandfather. He climbed, monkeylike, from Logan's arms into his father's. "I like it here a lot, Grandpa. And we'll come back for Christmas dinner, 'member? But there's more presents for me at home than here. I counted. So, I'm coming home as soon as your busys are finished, right, Dad?"

"Your what?" Logan's father asked.

"My *busys*, Cody calls them," Logan said. "You know. Things that come up now and then. Things that keep me too busy to have enough time for him. Like manuscript deadlines."

"Ahh..." His father gave him a worried look that wasn't at all tough to decipher.

It said that manuscript deadlines and chasing around after kidnappers were two entirely different things, and that his parents weren't the least bit impressed with what he'd gotten himself involved in. When they'd cornered him, out of Cody's hearing, he'd tried to get away with as little detail as possible about why he didn't want Cody at home. But they'd managed to drag enough out of him to become thoroughly alarmed.

"While you're poking around after those...those criminals," his father had snapped at one point, "just remember you're a writer, not Magnum, P.I., or Dirty Harry."

"Hey," his father was saying now, "I think we should let your dad get going, Cody—before it's too late for your grandmother to read you a bedtime story."

"Well...okay. Bye, Dad."

"Night, sport." Logan called another goodbye to his mother, then ruffled Cody's hair and opened the front door, saying, "You be good, and I'll talk to you in the morning."

When he walked out into the night, his thoughts immediately turned to Ali. It wasn't late. Barely eight o'clock. But in the dead of winter, like this, it was dark before six, and he hated the idea of her being alone in that big old house, with only her thoughts for company.

Navigating his way through the residential maze of Don Mills, he reached Lawrence and headed for the Parkway, his mind drifting back to the afternoon . . . to holding Ali and kissing her. She felt so incredibly right in his arms, as if she belonged in them. At least, that's how it felt from his side. He wasn't sure how it felt from hers.

She certainly hadn't rejected him. Far from it. Hell, just recalling how arousing her kisses had been was turning him on. But maybe, with the way things were, all she'd really wanted was to be held, to be close to someone. And he'd been right there—ready and willing.

God, so ready and willing it was unbelievable. He'd never felt this way about a woman before. His feelings for Loretta hadn't even come close. It might have taken him a long time to realize he was in love with Ali, but now that he had . . . well, all those months of biding his time and playing things cool had only made him want her more. Which got him back to the question of how *she* felt.

He could hardly press her to answer that question at the moment, though. Not under the circumstances. A horn blasted, telling him he was driving erratically, and he realized he'd made it onto the Parkway and almost all the way down to Bloor.

Pulling over to the right-hand lane, he flicked on the signal for his exit and let his thoughts drift back to Ali. What was going to happen when he went to L.A. next month? The answer was obvious, and he didn't like it. He'd go, but Ali would stay here.

She regretted having dropped out of university the first time, so she wouldn't make the same mistake again. And since she already had provisional acceptance to grad school next fall...

Of course, he might not be in California forever, but odds were he'd be gone a long time. His agent seemed certain he'd be asked to adapt the other two books that were optioned, and that could well lead to other projects. He reached the corner of Palmerston and turned down the quiet old street, deciding to leave the Jeep in his own drive, then walk along to Ali's—just make sure she was okay.

And then he saw it up ahead. Parked almost directly in front of his place, with a perfect view of Ali's, was the Caddy she'd told him about. Black, with dark windows that even in daylight would hide the interior from prying eyes.

Who was inside it? Nick Sinclair and Chico Gonzalez? Waiting to see if Bob Weyden came calling in the middle of the night? Pulling into his driveway, he climbed out of the Jeep and started back toward the street—feeling eyes watching him from behind those dark windows.

His initial impulse was to stop and knock on one of them, find out exactly who *was* in the car and what the hell they figured they were doing. Then he thought about the way Vinny Velarde had looked this morning. And about the fact that his father had been right. He was Logan Reed, writer, not Magnum, P.I., or Dirty Harry.

That took care of his initial impulse, but what other options did he have? He could phone the police. And what would he say? That he didn't like the looks of a car sitting outside his house? One parked in a perfectly legal space? Yeah, that would really get them here with their sirens screaming.

Realizing his options were extremely limited, he walked on by the Caddy—so preoccupied with it that he didn't notice, until he'd turned up Ali's walk, that there was only a single light on in the house.

It was upstairs, in her bedroom, and seeing that made him swear to himself. She liked to read in bed, so even though it was early she'd probably settled in for the night. Which meant she wouldn't appreciate company. But he was damned if he'd go home and leave her alone. Not with that car lurking.

For the first time in his life, he wished he had a gun, and that started him wondering if he'd buy one after he moved. From what he'd heard, everyone had them in L.A. But he wasn't in L.A. yet. He was still in Canada, where strict gun laws meant that ordinary citizens like him never had them. He glanced back at the Caddy, certain the guys inside weren't ordinary citizens.

That thought preying on his mind, he headed up Ali's front steps and turned the old knob that rang the bell, hoping he wasn't scaring her half to death. After a minute or so the stairway light came on and she appeared on the stairs, wearing her bunny slippers and a long fuzzy pink robe. It hid all her curves, yet somehow still managed to make her look sexy. She flicked on the porch light, saw it was him and smiled—a smile that went straight to his heart.

"Sorry," he said as she opened the door and gestured him inside. "I didn't want to get you up, but..."

"It's all right, I'm glad you did. I was trying to read, but I couldn't. In fact, I was just thinking about coming down and making hot chocolate. Want some?"

"Sure." What he really wanted was to take her in his arms, but something told him not to, so he simply turned and hung up his jacket while she headed for the kitchen. Then he just stood staring at the front door for a minute, wishing she had a solid steel one without a square inch of glass in it.

He'd never worried much about the doors in these old houses—had never even given them much thought before last night. But things were hardly the way they'd been before. Now things were scary as hell.

ABOVE THE LOW HUM of the microwave, Ali heard Logan heading down the hall. By the time she glanced across the room, he was standing in the kitchen doorway. Looking at him, she couldn't help remembering how comforting his arms had been this afternoon or how much better his kisses had made her feel—if only for a while.

And even though she was trying to see him objectively now, she was certain he had the most sensuous mouth in the entire world. The broadest shoulders, too—amazing, when he was essentially tall and lean. When you added in his chiseled features and deep, blue eyes, he was an exceptionally attractive man.

Just as her thoughts reached that point, he smiled at her. It was such a warm, easy smile that her objectivity slipped entirely away, and she began thinking that if her whole world wasn't turned upside down... She looked away from him. Her whole world *was* turned upside down and would be until Robbie was home. She might not regret having found comfort in Logan's arms once, but she wasn't going to be foolish.

They were good together as friends. Very good. So allowing their relationship to change would be very foolish indeed—particularly right now, when she was an emotional wreck and Logan was about to pack his bags for California.

He started across the kitchen. Then the microwave pinged, telling her the hot chocolate was ready, and she turned to get it.

"Was everyone glad to see you?" she asked a moment later, handing him one of the mugs and sitting down across from him.

"Uh-huh. And Cody's okay with staying there a little longer. How about you? You call Nancy back? And Bob's mother?"

"I tried Nancy, but I only got her machine. And Celeste...oh, Logan, I was too chicken to even try her. She's been through so much, thinking Bob was murdered and everything. She just doesn't need the stress of knowing Robbie's gone and all."

"She's going to find out what happened eventually."

Ali shrugged, knowing that was true. If *she* didn't tell Celeste, Robbie would be certain to—assuming he came through this fine. And if he didn't... She did her best to force away the fear that Robbie might never tell Celeste anything again.

"I just couldn't figure out what I'd say to her," she explained at last. "I mean, no matter what I thought of, it was going to come out sounding like a good-news-bad-news joke. The good news is that your son isn't really dead. But the bad news is that he's taken off with Robbie, and I'm scared to death I won't get him back safely."

"Ali, you *are* going to get him back safely. *We* are."

"You're right. We are." She had to keep believing that. And she had to stop thinking about Robbie every single second, because it was driving her crazy with worry.

Using all the mental energy she could summon, she managed to focus her thoughts on another subject. She was, she realized, becoming an expert at compartmentalizing everything in her mind and temporarily locking up the various compartments.

"You had a visitor while you were gone," she said. "She arrived when I was feeding Sammy."

"She?"

"Your wife."

"You mean my *ex*-wife," he said.

His expression revealed nothing more than mild surprise, but the way he emphasized the *ex* gave her a twinge of guilt. He'd *told* her he was divorced, and she'd never known him to lie. But when Loretta had distinctly said she was "Logan's wife..." Ali had been wondering about that off and on, although she didn't know why. What difference did it make to her whether

Logan and his *ex*-wife had bothered to legally finalize things?

"What did she want?" he asked at last.

"I . . . just to see you, as far as I could tell. And to see Cody."

"That would be a first," he muttered.

By taking a slow sip of hot chocolate, Ali managed not to ask what he meant by the remark. Both she and Logan liked to keep their private lives private. Before this afternoon, she hadn't even known Loretta's name. So as curious as she was about the woman, she didn't want to pry.

Well, that wasn't quite true. If she thought she could pry without seeming obvious, she would. But she couldn't think of any innocuous-sounding questions. When Logan remained silent, she tried volunteering more details. "She said she'll be in town until after New Year's Eve. And that she's staying at the Chelsea— She'd like you to call her."

Logan gave a noncommittal, "Hmm."

Ali ordered herself to keep quiet after that, but her curiosity eventually got the better of her. "She said she's here for a *gig*. At Bourbon Street, so I guess she must be good."

That elicited another "Hmm."

"I didn't even know she was a singer. You never mentioned that."

Logan caught Ali's gaze in the blue depth of his. "You want to hear the story, don't you?" he asked quietly.

She shrugged, as casually as she could. "I'm kind of curious."

"Yeah, well—" He raked his fingers through his hair, then sat staring at the table. "Okay, here's the short version," he muttered at last. "When Loretta and I met, she was trying to become the next Carly Simon, which meant spending a lot of time on the road. And I was hustling freelance articles to every editor who'd look at them, trying to pay the bills—and spending the rest of my time writing novels that publishers didn't want to buy. Neither of us was looking for anything permanent. Certainly not marriage."

"But?" Ali prompted when he paused.

"But we started seeing each other whenever she was in town and—hell, Ali, it's hard to explain how things were, because it's going to sound so shallow...."

She shrugged. "Who am I to pass judgment? Don't forget who I ended up married to."

That made Logan smile. "Well," he went on, "my point was that Loretta and I weren't desperately in love. We had fun together, but that was really the extent of it. And then ... well, then I got her pregnant."

"Ahh...so you did the right thing by her, as they used to say."

"No, that wasn't it. I mean, it wasn't that straightforward. She didn't want to marry me. She didn't want a husband and she *definitely* didn't want a baby—said a kid would be a death sentence to her career. So she'd gotten the name of a doctor in Buffalo..."

"Ahh," Ali murmured again. In her mother's day, back before abortions had been legal in Ontario, there'd been a special meaning to the phrase "shuffle off to Buffalo." A special meaning for unhappily pregnant women in Toronto, at least, with the New York State border only ninety miles away.

And even though the province had legalized abortions long before Robbie and Cody were born, there'd been an incredible amount of red tape involved in getting one. So a lot of women had still slipped down to Buffalo, rather than face a panel of Ontario doctors and try to convince them to approve the procedure.

"If Loretta'd had any money," Logan continued, "I don't think she'd even have told me she was pregnant. But she didn't have two cents, and I was the obvious one to help her get hold of some. When she told me, though... I mean, when she said she'd already decided on an abortion, I couldn't handle the idea."

Ali instinctively wrapped her arms around her stomach, knowing how she'd have felt if anyone had suggested an abortion when she'd been pregnant with Robbie. Suddenly thinking about him again brought tears to her eyes. She wiped them away before Logan saw them, but she was clearly still a long way from an *expert* at compartmentalizing her thoughts.

"My reaction surprised the hell out of me," Logan was saying, "because I'd always figured I was such a liberal thinker. But when it was *my* child we were talking about..."

"I understand."

"At any rate, I finally badgered Loretta into marrying me and having the baby. Told her she wouldn't have to look after it—that I could, because I worked at home most of the time. Promised her it wouldn't interfere with her career, that I wouldn't mind her still being on the road. And you know, I didn't.

"But... well, it didn't take me long to realize how unfair I'd been to her, forcing her into something she hadn't wanted. And it didn't take Loretta long to decide the whole charade was ridiculous. What we'd ended up with wasn't a marriage. It was Cody and me, and this woman who dropped in and stayed with us every now and then."

"Not exactly the perfect family."

"No, not anywhere near."

The guilt was audible in Logan's voice, but Ali knew if he had it to do over again he'd do the same thing. He'd no more look at Cody and feel he'd made a mistake than she'd look at Robbie and wish she hadn't met Bob.

"So it was no time at all," he was saying, "before Loretta said she wanted a divorce. Since then, she sends Cody presents on his birthday and at Christmas, but... well, I know it's because she feels she *should* keep in touch rather than because she really wants to. It's been over a year since we've actually seen her."

When Logan lapsed into another silence, Ali said, "You'll call her, though?"

"Yeah, I'll call her. But I won't set anything up with her until after you and I have got Robbie—"

The doorbell rang—cutting Logan off midsentence and starting Ali's heart pounding.

Chapter Nine

The sound of the doorbell died, but Ali just sat staring across the table at Logan, silently ordering her heart to stop racing. She wasn't expecting anyone and she'd had her fill of surprise visitors. She relaxed, though, when they headed out into the hall and saw it was Nancy McGuire on the porch.

"I guess," Ali said, "she's stopped by for an update."

"Be careful what you say," Logan murmured.

She nodded, but she didn't need reminding. As concerned as she knew Nancy was, she couldn't risk telling her much. Not when Nancy would repeat everything to Kent. Not when Kent would feel obliged to speak out if he knew Bob was after the insurance money.

"I'm not interrupting anything, am I?" Nancy asked when Ali opened the door.

"No, come on into the kitchen and—"

"Oh, thanks, but I can only stay a minute. Kent's working out of town this week and said he'd call me at ten. But I was catching up on things at the clinic, so

I thought I'd just check in on my way home—make sure you were okay and see where things stand."

"Well, I think everything's going to be all right. I talked to Robbie this morning and he's fine."

"But what's the story? Where's Bob been all this time? Did he know everyone thought he was dead? And taking Robbie like that—surely he doesn't want custody, does he?"

"I . . . Nancy, Bob said—"

"He doesn't want her talking about what's going on," Logan interrupted. "I know she'd like to tell you, but it's better if she doesn't. Not until after she and Bob have finished sorting things out and this is over. You understand."

Ali flashed him a look of gratitude for bailing her out.

"Yes, of course," Nancy said. "I just thought, if there was anything I could do to help . . ."

"Oh, I know," Ali said, giving her friend a quick hug. "And if there's anything I need, you're the first one I'll call."

"Well, all right. If you're sure there's nothing."

"Not right now. But thanks. Thanks so much."

Nancy opened the door and Ali started out onto the porch with her.

"Wait," Logan said. "Don't go out there with just your housecoat on. You'll freeze."

"I'll only be a second." She took another couple of steps, then stopped in her tracks. Over Nancy's shoulder she could see the black Caddy.

"What?" Nancy asked, eyeing her curiously. "What's the matter?"

"Nothing. The cold just hit me." She wrapped her arms around herself and pretended to shiver. "Go. I'll watch you to your car."

As Nancy headed over to the driveway, Ali turned to Logan. "You knew they were out here. You saw them earlier, didn't you?"

"Yeah, but I figured telling you would only give you another sleepless night."

She took a deep breath, trying to calm down. She'd almost managed to forget Nick Sinclair's promise to keep an eye on her, but there he was—sitting practically on her doorstep.

"Where do they think watching the house is going to get them?" she asked, glancing at Logan again. "Do they really figure Bob might come here? Because he won't."

"Then they're just wasting their time, aren't they," Logan said, even though he wasn't entirely convinced of that.

Nothing he'd heard about Bob Weyden added up to his being a normal, logical man. So maybe the idea of his coming by, for a final visit with Ali before he disappeared again, wasn't as improbable as she seemed to think. In fact, from all the research he'd done on the workings of the criminal mind, it wouldn't surprise him in the least.

That made him wonder if Ali was in denial about the possibility—to use one of her psychology terms. He didn't suggest that, though. He merely took her arm and drew her back inside. He didn't like the thought that Bob might show up any more than he liked the fact that the Caddy was sitting out there.

"Oh, Logan," she whispered as he locked the dead bolt. "What am I going to do? My life has turned into a bad TV movie. I've got killers watching my house, my son is heaven knows where and...and I feel stretched almost to the breaking point."

"You won't want to be alone, feeling like that," he murmured. "I'll stay the night again."

When she simply nodded, he didn't know what else to say, so he just flicked off the lights and held her. Once again, she felt absolutely perfect in his arms. And he couldn't keep from thinking back to the way she'd kissed him this afternoon—as if she hadn't wanted to stop at just kissing.

But if she felt stretched almost to the breaking point she couldn't really know *what* she wanted. So until she was off this emotional roller coaster Bob had put her on, Logan damned well wouldn't risk making things even more complicated for her.

He rested his chin lightly on the top of her head. Her hair was still cold from the air outside, but it smelled the way it always did—like a spring meadow. He loved the way she smelled. Hell, he loved everything about her. Even her shapeless fuzzy pink robe and stupid bunny slippers. But, he reminded himself, he wasn't going to make things more complicated. This just wasn't the time or place to take what he wanted.

Not even when he already had it right in his arms. Not even when he wanted her so badly it was making him ache.

LOGAN DIDN'T KNOW what had awakened him, and for a moment he didn't know where he was. Then the fog cleared from his brain and he remembered he'd stayed at Ali's again. The time panel glowing on the clock radio told him it was almost 3:00 a.m.

For a moment he just lay listening to the silence in the house, then he rolled out of bed and quietly crossed to the window. The guest room was at the front of the house, overlooking the street, and he automatically glanced in the direction of his own place.

Palmerston Boulevard had long ago tucked in for the night, and all the Christmas lights had been turned off. But there was the damned Caddy, still where it had been earlier. Just one car in the row parked along the street. He knew it wasn't really just one in the row, though. And he knew there still wasn't a damned thing he could do about its being there.

He stood watching it...thinking how convinced Ali was that the guys inside were wasting their time... thinking that she was probably right. She knew Bob a whole lot better than Nick Sinclair did, so if she figured there was no way he'd be visiting her, he likely wouldn't. Then, just as Logan was about to head back to bed, a car came crawling along the street from the other direction.

He focused on it. A light-colored Accord...no, it was a Taurus, moving so slowly that the driver might be checking house numbers. Logan's adrenaline started pumping. Normally, in the middle of the night, there was no traffic at all on this street.

By the time the Taurus was in front of Ali's, it had slowed almost to a stop. Then it pulled into the row of parked cars, into the space across the end of her driveway, and stopped. Seconds later the headlights went out, the interior light came on, and the driver's door opened.

A man climbed out, and the glow from the street-lights was enough to give Logan a good look at him. He guessed the guy was in his late forties. And also guessed he was Bob Weyden. Ali had been wrong and Nick Sinclair had been right.

Bob stood slowly gazing along the street, his car door still open and the engine still running. Logan couldn't hear it through the closed window, but he could see the exhaust puffing into the cold night air like a tiny, ground-level cloud. He glanced from Bob to the Caddy, knowing he should do something but not knowing what.

And then it was too late.

Almost in the same instant, the front doors of the Caddy flew open, two figures emerged from it, and Bob Weyden dove back inside his car. The next moment the Taurus was racing in reverse, back down the street the way it had come, its engine revving loudly enough that Logan could hear it from inside.

When Logan glanced back at the Caddy, he realized the two men had scrambled inside it again. When it wheeled out of its space, it caught the bumper of the car in front, hard enough that he heard *that* sound, as well. Then, with no room to turn around on the narrow street, the Caddy's driver roared off in reverse—after the Taurus.

His adrenaline pumping harder yet, Logan watched until the cars had disappeared. With his head start, Bob would make it to College before the Caddy did. But then what?

What if Nick Sinclair caught up with him? What if Bob Weyden was suddenly out of the picture? If he was no longer around, issuing orders to whoever had Robbie, what would happen to *him?*

It was the first question that would occur to Ali ... assuming he told her what he'd just seen. So what was he going to do come morning? Tell her or not? He wandered back over to the bed and lay staring into the darkness, finally deciding he wouldn't. Not right away, at any rate.

The decision raised a few pangs of guilt. If he was in her shoes, he'd want to know every single thing that was relevant—wouldn't want anyone holding back anything from him.

But *he* wasn't in her shoes, *she* was. And he had a feeling that anything more to worry about would push her beyond that breaking point she was so close to.

WHEN LOGAN WAS STILL on the phone to Cody at eight-forty the next morning, Ali began to get anxious, wishing he'd clear the line. But after he did, the phone was silent.

By ten past nine, she was certain she was never going to hear from Robbie again. Then the phone rang, the red light on the tape recorder lit up, and her son was on the line.

"Oh, darling," she said, desperately trying to sound normal. "I'm so happy to hear your voice. I've been missing you so much."

"I miss you, too, Mommy. So can you come get me today?"

"Darling . . . darling, I wish I could, but you're going to have to stay there for just a little while longer."

"But why? I don't wanna."

She swallowed hard, hearing the tears in his voice. Logan reached across the table and patted her hand. It helped, but not nearly enough.

"That's a hard *why*, Robbie," she managed to say.

"So hard that I can't explain it over the phone. But once you're home—"

"But *when*, Mommy? *When* can I come home?"

"Well . . . darling, I think maybe you'll have to stay there until Friday."

"Is that tomorrow?"

"No, it's not *quite* tomorrow."

She heard him choke back a sob and hurried on, hoping he couldn't tell she was frantic with worry. "Tomorrow's Wednesday, Robbie. And after that there's only Thursday left before Friday. It's not really so very long."

"Is it before Christmas?"

"Yes, darling, it's before Christmas. You'll be home for Christmas."

"But what if I'm not? Mommy, what's gonna happen to my presents if I'm not there to open them?"

"You will be, darling. I'll make sure you are."

"But what if I'm not? Santa won't know where to find me, Mommy. He won't know I'm here."

Ali held her breath, half *afraid* he'd say something more about where "here" was, half *hoping* he would. If he did, Bob might make good on his threat not to let her talk to him again. But if he said enough . . .

"Mommy?" he whispered.

"What?" she whispered back.

"Mommy, I hate it here. She's mean to me."

"Gimme that phone" a voice growled in the background. A second later, the line went dead.

"Oh, my God," Ali whispered. "Oh, my God."

"What?" Logan demanded.

She shook her head and handed him the phone, unable to get another word out.

He listened for an instant. Only long enough, she imagined, to hear there was nothing but a dial tone, then he rewound the tape and played it.

"She," he said when it finished. *"She.* And that sounded like a woman's voice, didn't it?"

Ali nodded numbly. A man had taken Robbie. Cody had seen a man. But Robbie had just said *she.* And that *had* sounded like a woman's voice. So how many people did Bob have helping him? And who was the *she?*

"The voice," Logan was saying. "Did it sound at all familiar?"

"No."

He fiddled with the tape, then played the last bit a second time. "You're sure?"

She nodded again.

"Well, even so, now we know that wherever Robbie is, he's with a woman."

"A *mean* woman," Ali whispered, her throat still so tight she could barely speak. "Oh, Lord, what's this doing to him, Logan? What if he ends up scarred for life? What if...?"

"Ali, don't," he said, reaching over and taking both her hands in his. "He's not going to be scarred for life.

Kids are resilient as hell. And you know what *he* says is mean might not count for anything. Maybe the woman hasn't baked any cookies. That would be enough to make her mean in *his* books. But this is what we were hoping for—a clue."

Ali silently held his gaze and he realized she was waiting for him to go on, to tell her what *use* the clue was.

He swore to himself. He had no idea, but he couldn't make himself say that. She was counting on him to know what he was doing. After all, how many times had he told her they were going to make things turn out fine?

"All right," he said at last, looking across the table at her again. "Let's try to figure things out. Let's assume we were wrong about Vinny and—"

"*I* was wrong, you mean," Ali murmured. "*I* was the one who said it had to be him."

"Hey, it still could be. Maybe he was lying through his teeth yesterday. But let's just try considering other possibilities, okay?"

When she nodded, he went on. "Okay, let's start with this. Aside from Vinny, who knew you'd be taking Robbie to that party?"

"Nobody," she said after a moment.

"Ali, are you *sure?* You didn't mention it to *anyone* except him?"

She pushed her hair back from her face, saying, "The only other person I remember telling is Celeste. But she's crazy about Robbie. She'd never, ever—"

"*Celeste?* Bob's *mother?* You're saying Bob's *mother* knew you were going?"

"Yes, but—"

"Whoa. Just hold on a minute." He rewound the tape again and played it a third time.

"Gimme that phone" the voice said once more.

"You're positive," he asked, "that couldn't have been Celeste's voice?"

"No. I mean, the way it was just a hiss, I guess it could have been almost anyone. But Celeste would never say *gimme* like that."

"Okay," Logan said, rubbing his jaw. "That doesn't mean she's not involved, though."

"Logan, she isn't anything like Bob. She's a typical doting grandmother and she'd *never* go along with something that would upset Robbie, so—"

"Wait. Just let me think out loud for a minute, because you know this story a lot better than I do. Celeste thought Bob was dead, right? The same as everyone else?"

"Yes . . . yes, I've never even wondered about that before, but she *had* to. She was so brokenhearted. Even now she still...no, it can't possibly have been an act."

"Okay, then, we've got a woman who thinks her son is dead. Then she suddenly hears from him. But he tells her that unless she helps him he really *is* going to be dead—that a couple of goons are trying to kill him, and he needs your two million bucks to get away from them.

"So where does that leave her? What does she do if she has to choose between her grandson being upset for a few days and her son being dead?"

"Oh, Lord," Ali whispered. "It sounds so logical when you put it like that."

Logan leaned back in his chair, glancing absently across the room. Then something clicked in his mind and he focused on the party invitation that was still on the fridge door.

"Nancy," he said, looking back at Ali. "You told me Nancy invited you to the party."

"Well, yes, but—"

"And she knows Bob?"

"Yes, but—"

"And that voice? The woman with Robbie?"

"No! Nancy would no more say *gimme* than Celeste would."

"Okay...okay, so he's not with either of them. Which makes sense. Even if one of them *is* part of this, that would be too risky. You could easily show up at either of their places, right?"

Ali nodded.

"Okay, then, let's say the woman is just somebody Bob's got taking care of Robbie. But either Celeste or Nancy could have... What about Kent? Would Nancy have told him you were going to that party? Mentioned it ahead of time, I mean?"

Logan waited impatiently for Ali's answer, his excitement growing. Things were looking a whole lot better. One of these people *had* to be the key.

"I'm not sure if Nancy would have said anything, but..." Ali pressed her fingers to her mouth as the pieces suddenly fell into place. Logan's question about Kent had started a scene from the Christmas party replaying in her head.

"But?" he prompted.

"At the party. When Robbie was on your knee. I'd just started across the back of the room, to wait for him, when Kent stopped me. And by the time I'd finished talking to him, Robbie was gone."

"You think that was part of a plan, then? You think Kent's the one?"

"Yes...no. Oh, Logan, I'm getting so confused I don't know what to think. For a second that seemed to add up, but it can't be Kent. He never even met Bob."

Logan swore silently. He'd figured they had it and they didn't. Not yet. But *something* had to add up. "Okay, go back to when Kent stopped you, and tell me the details. What did he say? Was Nancy with him?"

"No. He said she'd gone to her office for something."

"You mean she was out of the room? When Robbie was grabbed?"

"It was a man who took him," she said, not certain Logan was suggesting what he seemed to be. "It couldn't have been Nancy, because Cody saw a man."

"I know, but—okay, go on. Kent stopped you and said...?"

"Something about suspecting that Nancy was involved with somebody else. And that he thought I'd know whether she was."

"And is she?"

"I don't think so. Not that she's told me about, at least. But Kent said—I can't remember exactly—oh, he'd overheard bits of some phone calls she'd gotten, that was it. And he thought there was something strange going on—something she didn't want to talk about it in front of him. He seemed sure there was *something* Nancy was keeping from him.''

"Something like she was helping Bob plan a kidnapping?" Logan said.

Chapter Ten

An hour later, they were still going around in circles.

Logan paced back across the living room, then sank onto the couch beside Ali, saying, "Okay, let's go through this one more time. Could be we've been missing something critical."

She nodded, although they'd already gone over everything so many times she couldn't believe they'd missed even the tiniest detail. And she also couldn't believe either Celeste or Nancy had teamed up with Bob.

Of course, she knew part of the problem was that she didn't want to believe it. Because if she considered *only* the logic of the situation, she knew one of them must have. Unless Vinny really *had* been lying through his teeth, either Nancy or Celeste had told Bob about that party.

Nancy had been her friend for years, though. And even if Logan's hypothesis was right...

"Maybe," he'd suggested a while ago, "Bob offered her a share of the insurance money if she helped him out." But the idea of Nancy going along with a proposal like that seemed inconceivable—even if Bob had offered her the entire two million.

The thought of Robbie's grandmother helping kidnap him seemed almost as incredible. Still, Celeste would have been helping kidnap him for his own father. She could have convinced herself that he'd be perfectly safe with Bob. So, possibly...

"Okay," Logan said, "the only reason we've been assuming a *man* took Robbie is because of what Cody said. But all he really saw was an arm. And a hand in a glove. So it could easily have been a woman, wearing a man's coat and gloves. Or maybe Cody only *thought* the clothes were a man's."

"And Robbie would have gone with either Nancy or Celeste without making a fuss," Ali murmured, feeling as if she had her lines memorized by this point.

"And if it was Nancy, then she probably got Kent involved—asked him to stop you to give her the time she needed. Otherwise, it would have been one hell of a coincidence, wouldn't it?"

"I... yes, it would." She closed her eyes for a moment, hoping it would help clear her head. Every time she started thinking it just might be one of them, Logan seemed to be thinking it was the other. "You're leaning toward Nancy, then?" she asked at last.

Logan hesitated, then said, "No, actually I'm not. Coincidences *do* happen. And Celeste is a more obvious bet. After all, we keep coming back to the fact that Bob would have told her she'd be helping save his life. And that would be motivation for a mother to do just about anything."

"Yes, anything," Ali murmured, thinking how much she'd do to save *her* son's life. "So, if Celeste's the more likely one, where do we go from here?"

"I think you should pay her a visit."

"Me? You mean alone?"

"Uh-huh. She'd be less open if you brought a stranger along. But you think she's home now?"

"Yes, probably."

"Then you should just drop in unannounced and see what reactions you get—one-on-one, face-to-face."

"But what if I don't get any further with her than we did with Vinny?"

"Then we'll try Nancy. We're going to get to the bottom of this, Ali."

She gazed at him, desperately wanting to believe what he was saying.

"And we're going to do it fast," he added firmly. "While you're seeing Celeste, I'll check around and find out what I can about Kent."

"But he's out of town, remember? Nancy mentioned that last night."

"Well, I can find out a lot about him regardless of where he is. And if it turns out he really *isn't* out of town, after Nancy said he was..."

"You think she was lying?"

"Who knows. But we can't chance taking anything we're told at face value."

"I hate this," Ali said, as much to herself as to Logan. "I hate that somebody has my son and I hate not knowing how to get him back. I hate that this is like a big puzzle with a bunch of the pieces missing. And I hate that I'm suspecting my friends of doing something so unspeakably awful. I just . . . oh, I just want this to be over and Robbie to be home. Is that wanting too terribly much?'' Her eyes began swimming with tears and she tried to blink them away.

Logan draped his arm over her shoulders and pulled her close. "It's *going* to be over," he murmured against her hair. "And Robbie's going to be home. But right this minute, we don't know who or what we can believe. So we're just going to have to poke around until we hit pay dirt. You can handle that, Ali."

She took a deep breath and told herself he was right. She *could* handle it. And she would. In just a minute or two, she'd go upstairs and get ready to visit Celeste.

But she was so frightened for Robbie. Just so frightened. And it felt so warm and safe in Logan's embrace that she wished she could stay right where she was forever.

Then she guiltily thought about how alone Robbie must feel. There was no one holding *him* close. No one making him feel warm and safe—not even for a minute.

The image of the little boy she loved, all on his own, brought fresh tears to her eyes.

ALI PULLED INTO Celeste's driveway, cut the engine, then simply sat staring at the house. A rambling ranch-style, it was far too big for one person. But Celeste hadn't sold it after Bob's father had died, almost ten years ago, and now she lived here with only her memories.

Inside, framed photographs were everywhere. They covered the top of the baby grand she still played, the dressers in the bedrooms, and every other likely surface. Most were pictures of her husband, of Bob and of Robbie.

"I just can't bear to think about selling," she always said, and Ali could understand why. It was a welcoming sort of house.

Right now, though, it was one of the last places on earth she'd be if she had a choice. She'd spent the entire drive over trying to think of what she should say, but she still hadn't even come up with a good opening line.

"Play it by ear," Logan had said—far from the most helpful advice he'd ever given her.

She made herself get out of the car and start for the front door, her thoughts spinning. It would be one thing if she was *certain* Bob had asked his mother for help. Certain that Celeste knew he was alive. But it was entirely possible she didn't.

As far as Ali knew, Celeste had never suspected her son was anything but an upstanding citizen. She'd thought the sun rose and set on Bob, and he'd always relished that. So, given the way his mind worked, the last thing he'd want to do was tarnish his mother's image of him. And telling her he'd faked his death and was holding Robbie for ransom would certainly have done that.

Which meant Bob would have been pretty desperate before he'd have contacted Celeste. Of course, he *was* desperate, so maybe he *had* turned to her for help. And if he had, maybe Celeste had been persuaded to go along with his scheme. As Logan had said, helping save her child's life would motivate a mother to do just about anything.

Ali hesitated at the door, unable to make herself ring the bell. She wasn't a detective and she didn't have any idea how to go about this. If there wasn't so much at stake, she'd turn and run. Then the door opened and it was too late to do anything but proceed.

"Why, Ali," Celeste said, "what a surprise." She smiled to show it was a welcome one, and pushed back a wisp of white hair that had escaped her usually perfect French knot.

Ali eyed her closely, but Celeste looked exactly as she always did. She could easily have been on her way to audition for a modeling job with a seniors fashion magazine.

"I heard the car," she went on, her smile deepening the little lines around her blue eyes. "And I've been waiting for a delivery so I thought that's what it was. But you're alone, dear?" she asked, peering out toward the driveway. "Robbie's not with you? He still has school this week?"

"Yes . . . yes, the break doesn't start until Thursday."

"Oh, well, come in out of the cold. I'm afraid the living room's a mess. I'm just in the midst of wrapping presents and . . . oh, now that you're here I can show you the darling Blue Jays uniform I got Robbie. He's going to look exactly like a little ball player in it."

Ali tried to smile but couldn't. It had taken all of sixty seconds for instinct to tell her Celeste hadn't heard from Bob. The desire to turn and run came back full force. But yesterday, she'd been positive that Vinny was their man. So she couldn't trust her instincts. Like it or not, she was going to have to make absolutely certain that Celeste wasn't their woman.

She followed along into the living room, and when Celeste began rummaging through the pile of unwrapped presents she took the opportunity to glance around—hoping something strange would leap out at her. Nothing did.

She could see only two things that were different. A Christmas tree was standing in front of the baby grand, its branches hiding that particular collection of photographs. And, as Celeste had said, the living room was a mess—according to *her* standards, at least. Normally there wasn't a thing out of place. Today, the carpet was littered with wrapping paper and ribbon.

"Here it is," Celeste said, holding up a little Blue Jays uniform. "Isn't this the sweetest thing you ever saw?"

Ali forced a smile. "Robbie will love it."

"And look," Celeste said, turning it back to front. "Number twelve.

"That's Robbie Alomar's number," she elaborated when Ali stared blankly. "Robbie Alomar...Robbie Weyden."

"He'll *really* love it."

"I know. The salesclerk told me she gave one to *her* grandson for his birthday and he wants to wear it all the time. He even tried to wear it to bed one night. They didn't have such darling things when Bob was a

little boy. The only cute outfit I can remember..."
Celeste paused, her eyes glistening.

"Sorry," she said, quickly wiping them. "I know
it's been a long time now but...they say losing a child
is the worst thing that can happen to a woman, and I
think they're right. Even when it's an adult child.
And—Ali, I know I don't say things like this very often—not often enough, I'm sure. But I'm so glad
Robbie's still in my life. Robbie *and* you, dear."

Ali's throat was suddenly tight and her own eyes
filled with tears. Why didn't she just turn around and
walk out of here without saying a word about either
Bob or Robbie? Celeste hadn't played any part in
Bob's plan. That was perfectly obvious. And once
Robbie was safely home, what had happened wouldn't
seem so horrific. It would be easier on Celeste to hear
about it after the fact.

An imaginary voice whispered that Robbie might
never be safely home, but Ali closed her ears to it. He
would be. So what was the point in making Celeste
frantic with worry now? She considered that for a
moment, then reminded herself how much was at
stake. She couldn't risk even the slightest chance that
what seemed perfectly obvious might not be.

She looked back at Celeste, who was carefully re-
folding the little uniform, and cleared her throat.

"Would you like some tea?" Celeste asked, glancing at her. "Or coffee?"

"No, but there's something I have to talk to you
about. Would you mind sitting down for a minute?"

"Oh, dear," Celeste murmured, looking crest-
fallen. "There's a problem with Christmas dinner,

isn't there. I suspected that when you didn't call me back yesterday. But if something's come up it's all right. You know my friend, Margie? Next door? Well, she invites me to go there every year and—"

"No, it isn't about Christmas dinner."

Celeste hesitated, then sat down on the couch.

Ali sank into one of the chairs that faced it, still vainly searching for the right words.

Even though Celeste was in good health, she was seventy-three years old. Hearing that her dead son wasn't actually dead might be enough to give her a stroke all by itself, without the added news that he'd taken Robbie.

"What is it, Ali?" Celeste asked, concern creeping into her voice. "What's wrong? Is it Robbie? Is he ill?"

"No...no, he's not ill but...someone took him. On Sunday. While we were at that Christmas party I told you we were going to."

"Took him?" Celeste whispered, her face growing whiter than her hair. "You mean kidnapped him?"

"Well, it was sort of a kidnapping, but not exactly. It was someone I know."

"Ali, I don't understand. *What* are you saying?"

"Celeste, this is going to shock you, but...Bob isn't actually dead. He faked his death because—because he was in trouble. And he couldn't let anyone know he was really alive. Not even you." Celeste began to tremble, so Ali quickly moved to the couch beside her and took her hands.

"That can't be true," Celeste finally whispered.

"It is. I've talked to him. He phoned me."

"Alive," Celeste murmured. "But...no. No, that isn't right. If Bob was alive, he'd have phoned *me*, Ali."

Her heart began aching for Celeste. Seeing the woman's reaction made her even more certain she'd known nothing. But now that she'd started explaining, she had to finish.

"Celeste, it *was* Bob. But because of this trouble he's in, he's going to have to disappear again. And he thought it would be better if everyone just went on believing he's dead. That's why he didn't phone you. He's never going to be able to see you again, so he thought— He's doing what he felt was best for you."

"He felt it was best for me not to know he's alive? To go on thinking my only son is dead?"

Celeste's pain was palpable, and the tears trickling down her cheeks almost started Ali crying as well.

"But why, Ali?" she whispered. "If he doesn't want *anyone* to know he's alive, why did he tell you? If he contacted someone, why wasn't it me?"

"Because *he* was the one who took Robbie," Ali made herself say. "He wants the insurance money from me, and he took Robbie to make me give it to him."

"No," Celeste whispered. "Oh, no, Bob would never do anything like that. Ali, you must be wrong. Somebody else phoned you, pretending to be Bob. Somebody else took Robbie. Somebody else wants the money from you. That has to be it. But what's going to happen? What's going to happen to Robbie?"

Celeste's voice had taken on a sharp edge of hysteria, so Ali squeezed her hands tightly and said, "Just listen to me. Listen to what I'm saying. It *wasn't* somebody else. I spoke to him three separate times, and it was *definitely* Bob. And because it was, I'm going along with what he wants and just praying Robbie will be fine.

"I...Celeste, I'm sorry. I'm so, so sorry I had to tell you this. But it's not *all* bad, is it? Your son is alive. So even though you won't be able to see him, doesn't knowing that he isn't dead..." Her words trailed off as Celeste pulled her hands free and furiously waved her away—tears streaming down her face now.

Ali edged off the couch and backed across the room, not knowing what to do. Turning to the window, she glanced past her car to the house next door. That was where Celeste's friend, Margie, lived. So maybe she should run over there and...

Her gaze came to rest on the baby grand. Now that she was standing beside the tree its branches weren't blocking her view of the piano.

Sensing there was something different about it, she mentally inventoried the photographs on display and realized one was missing.

The school picture of Robbie she'd given Celeste only a month ago.

"ARE YOU *POSITIVE?*" Logan demanded, grabbing a couple of mugs from Ali's cupboard—so fiercely she thought he'd pull the handles off. "You're *positive* she hadn't realized the picture was gone?"

Ali made a helpless little gesture with her hand. She *was* positive, but it was clear that Logan didn't want to believe her, didn't want to eliminate Celeste as a possibility.

"I'm as positive as I can be," she finally said. "Logan, by the time I noticed that picture was missing, the poor woman was practically hysterical. She swore she had no idea what had happened to it, and I believed her. I think Bob just went in and took it."

"Without leaving any sign of a break-in?"

"She keeps a spare key in the garage, and he knows where she hides it. He knows she never misses church on Sunday morning, too, so he could easily have slipped in and out then."

Logan ran his fingers through his hair and stared out into the gathering darkness.

He looked so upset that Ali could tell he was thinking along the same lines she was. Another day was almost gone, and they were no further ahead than they'd been on Sunday. How were they ever going to find Robbie when Bob had thought about every single detail? Right down to getting a recent photograph, so that whoever was supposed to take Robbie would be sure to get *him*, not one of the other little boys at the party.

"I really don't think," she finally murmured, "that there's even the slightest chance Celeste knew Bob was alive. You didn't see her, Logan. I felt . . . I just felt so awful about what I was doing to her."

"Hey," he said quietly. "This whole thing's awful, and you only did what you had to. I guess I was getting pretty short with you there, but I didn't mean to.

It's just that when I didn't find anything at Kent's, I was hoping to hell you'd gotten someplace with Celeste."

"It's okay. I know."

"Well...look, I'm going to call Cody, okay? Just check in with him before we go to Nancy's?"

"Sure." Ali turned back to the coffeemaker as Logan reached for the phone, and she tried not to think how much she wished she could simply dial a number and talk to Robbie.

"Hi, Dad," Logan said after a minute. "Cody behaving himself?'

Not wanting to listen, Ali stood watching the coffee trickling down through the filter and reviewing what they'd learned today. Or, rather, what they hadn't learned.

Kent, Logan had established, really *was* working out of town this week. And when Logan had "checked out" his apartment, he'd turned up nothing even slightly suspicious. Definitely nothing for them to follow up on. Absently, she wondered again how Logan had gotten in. But when she'd asked, all he'd said was that he'd picked up some useful tricks while doing research for his books—and that he'd just as soon she'd forget about his bending the law.

Of course, it wasn't how he'd gotten into Kent's apartment that mattered. The important thing was that he'd found nothing helpful. Which left them with only one suspect. And if they drew a blank with *her*...

Ali pushed her hair back from her face, not wanting to even think about that. A few hours ago, she'd been certain Nancy couldn't have had anything to do with taking Robbie. Now she'd reached the stage of hoping Nancy had been in it up to her eyebrows. If they were ever going to learn where Robbie was, they had to get a lead from *somebody*. The trickle of coffee had slowed to an irregular drip, so Ali switched off the maker, thinking that even though she wasn't much of a drinker, she'd far prefer a gin and tonic. A very stiff one.

But she wanted her head clear in case... well, for *whatever* happened next.

Chapter Eleven

While Nancy was taking their jackets, Logan gave Ali a thumbs-up for encouragement. It didn't make her feel even slightly encouraged. She just hadn't been able to convince herself they were going to learn anything more useful from Nancy than they had from either Vinny or Celeste—or from Kent's apartment, for that matter.

"Well, let's go sit down," Nancy said, turning from the closet.

In jeans and a sweatshirt, instead of one of her social-worker-style suits, and with her hair loose, instead of pulled back the way she wore it to work, she looked very young. Very young and very innocent, Ali thought morosely. No movie director in his right mind would ever cast her as a kidnapper's accomplice.

When they reached the living room, Nancy gestured Ali and Logan to the couch, then sat down across from them, saying, "So, can you let me in on what's happening yet, or is Bob still telling you not to say anything?"

"Actually," Ali said, "there's not much to let you in on. Bob still has Robbie and...well, the longer this goes on, the more worried I'm getting."

"Of course," Nancy murmured. "Of course you are."

Ali glanced unhappily at Logan. When they'd planned their strategy, they'd decided she'd do the talking and he'd concentrate on Nancy's reactions. But now that the time had come to talk, she didn't know if she was up to it. Nancy was an intelligent woman. She would be bound to realize they suspected her, no matter how hard Ali worked at not letting it sound that way.

"So," she forced herself to go on, "what we're trying to do— Nancy, I have to ask you about something you're going to think is crazy, but..."

"But—?"

"But somebody who knows me helped Bob take Robbie, and—"

"Somebody *helped* him? Oh, Ali, who?"

"That's what we're trying to figure out. It had to be one of the people who knew Robbie and I were going to that party, because *somebody* told Bob we'd be there."

"Ahh," Nancy said. "There couldn't have been many of us who knew."

It was a simple statement of fact that didn't sound even slightly defensive, and Ali realized Nancy had just slipped into her social worker mode. So much for Logan's reading anything from her reactions. Nancy's face had become a mask of calm, revealing nothing. She sat back in her chair and quietly waited for someone else to fill the silence. One of the "helping profession" tricks she'd totally perfected.

"You're right." Ali continued even though it seemed entirely futile. "Only a few people knew Robbie would be at the party. So we've been talking to them and... and I've been wondering about something Kent did there."

"Kent?" Nancy said, a flicker of surprise crossing her face.

Ali nodded, suddenly hopeful they hadn't reached *entirely* futile after all. Asking about Kent, instead of a question Nancy would logically have expected, seemed to have thrown her a little.

"Nancy," she pressed on quickly, "when Robbie disappeared, I mean the exact minute he disappeared, Kent was talking to me."

"Well, we *were* all sitting together."

"Not right then. Robbie was with Logan... with Logan playing Santa, that is. And I was on my way over to get him when he finished. But before I got there, Kent stopped me."

"I don't remember that."

"No, you'd gone someplace. Kent said you'd gone to your office for something."

Nancy eyed her for a moment, then slowly said, "And you want to know if I really had? If that's *actually* where I was? Ali, you don't *really* think I might have helped Bob, do you?"

"No, I...Nancy, no. I'm sorry about how awful this seems, but I'm so upset, and I don't know who I can believe."

"I know," Nancy said quietly, leaning forward. "It's all right. You're under an incredible amount of stress, and you want to do everything you can to get Robbie back. But let's think about this rationally for a minute. I'm one of your best friends. And Kent is...he's one of the most honest people I've ever met."

"Nancy, the point is—" Logan began.

"No." She waved at him to be quiet, then focused on Ali again. "Ali, with all the psychology you've taken, you've got to know a situation like this can make people totally paranoid. They start thinking crazy thoughts and jumping to wrong conclusions—it makes them grasp at any straw blowing in the wind.

"So, look, Ali, I don't know who else *could* have told Bob you'd be at the party, but are you even sure that *anybody* did? I mean, did Bob *tell* you somebody did, or are you just guessing?"

"Well, no, he didn't *tell* me but—"

"Then couldn't he have just been following you around or something? Waiting for an opportunity to take Robbie?"

Cold, clammy fingertips began inching their way up Ali's spine. She could recall Logan saying practically the same thing on Sunday night.

"I just assumed," he'd said, "Bob had been watching the house and followed you to the clinic. But that snatch was so damned smooth maybe he *couldn't* have set it up on the spur of the moment."

Maybe he couldn't have. But he certainly could have if he'd been acting alone, if he hadn't had to set things up beforehand, with somebody else. If, despite what he'd told her, it had been *him* who'd taken Robbie—not some stranger he'd hired.

They only had Bob's word that he didn't want Robbie to know he was alive, that he wasn't going to let Robbie see him. And Bob's word wasn't worth two cents.

So maybe she and Logan had been wasting their time for the past two days. Maybe nobody but Bob knew anything about where Robbie was. Nobody but Bob and the *mean* woman.

Logan reached for Ali's hand. Her face had grown pale and she seemed to have suddenly run out of steam, so he decided he'd better try to pick up the conversation—although he doubted it was going to get them anywhere. Either Nancy was as innocent as she seemed, or she was far too cool a customer to let them rattle her. But if there was *anything* they could find out from her, the only way to do it was to get her talking.

"We weren't really thinking you or Kent had anything to do with what happened," he ventured. "But what Ali started to tell you was that Kent asked her about something that—well, the conversation's been bothering her."

"Oh?" Nancy met his gaze and held it.

"Yes," Ali said.

Logan glanced at her again and squeezed her hand. She looked as if she'd managed to pull herself together a bit.

"Nancy," she continued, "Kent wanted to know if I thought you were involved with someone else."

"Good grief," Nancy murmured. "You mean he actually asked you?"

"Uh-huh. He said you'd told him he should. But both the question and his timing seemed...peculiar."

"Good grief," Nancy said again. "I guess it *would* seem peculiar. But I *did* tell him to ask you. While you were in line with the boys, he made some dumb remark about the *other man* in my life. And I thought he was being such an idiot that I told him to ask you for the truth—since he obviously didn't believe me. But I didn't think he really would. He must have been more worried about it than I realized."

"So there's no one?"

"No, of course not. I'm crazy about Kent. You know that."

"But he said you'd been getting phone calls from some man."

"Well...yes, that's what got him going. Because I wouldn't tell him who it was. But the *man* is a caterer. Kent's thirtieth birthday is next month and I'm planning a surprise party. In fact, I intended to invite you when I saw you on Sunday—as soon as I had a chance when he wasn't around.

"You're still not sure you can believe me, are you?" she added after a moment.

When Ali hesitated, Nancy pushed herself out of her chair and headed over to her desk. "How about if I show you the caterer's contract? And the guest list?"

"I'LL BE UP IN A MINUTE or so," Logan said. "I'm just going to double-check the locks."

Ali merely nodded, then started for the stairs.

Logan anxiously followed her with his eyes. Tonight, he hadn't even bothered asking whether she wanted him to stay. She was so emotionally fragile he'd never have left her on her own. Once he heard her reach the second floor, he headed to the door and took a long look out at the street.

There was no black Caddy parked within sight of the house, but he hadn't really expected it would be. After last night, Nick Sinclair would know it was pointless to stake out Ali's house any longer. Bob Weyden wouldn't even think about coming around again. Of course, that was assuming Sinclair and his buddy hadn't managed to catch up with him. If they *had,* Bob probably wouldn't be thinking about *anything.*

Still staring into the darkness, Logan began wondering again how that crazy reverse chase scene had ended . . . and wondering again what would happen to Robbie if Sinclair *did* catch up with Bob before he sent the boy home . . . if Bob had ever *intended* to send Robbie home, that was.

What, exactly, had Wes Penna said?

It didn't take much effort to recall. "He doesn't exactly sound like father of the year. I sure wouldn't count on him worrying about what happens to anyone but himself."

And having Sinclair hot on his tail was going to make Bob even more desperate just to get that money and run. So what *would* end up happening to Robbie? Wearily, Logan turned and started for the stairs, thinking there were too many unknowns and too few knowns. Hell, there were almost no knowns at all.

After two full days of trying to find a decent clue, they hadn't come up with anything except that woman's voice—which had done absolutely nothing for them. And he knew Ali was even closer to the breaking point than she'd been before. She hadn't said a word during the drive back from Nancy's. Not a single word. And neither had he. What was there to say when he was straight out of ideas?

He reached the top of the stairs and headed along toward the front of the house, pausing when he reached Ali's bedroom. Her door was open, the bedside light was on, and she was sitting up in bed, just staring at the phone on the night table. She was wearing a silky white nightshirt, and her face was almost as pale as the fabric. She looked so vulnerable he wanted to take her in his arms and never let her go.

Instead, he just stood in the doorway, waiting for her to notice him. When she finally glanced over, her eyes were a darker brown than normal—shining with tears.

"How you doing?" he asked, even though it was a dumb question.

"I've been better," she said softly. "I just can't stop worrying about Robbie, not for a single minute. Worrying about where he is and how frightened he has to be and what he must have been thinking all day. Logan, he's got to be thinking I don't love him enough to come and get him, that..."

Logan walked slowly over and sat down on the edge of the bed. "No, that's not it at all. He *knows* how much you love him, so I'll bet he was thinking about what you told him this morning. That he'll be home in just a little while—in time for Christmas."

"But will he?" she whispered.

"Yeah . . . yeah, he will."

"And will he be the same happy little boy after he's been through this?"

"Sure he will. He'll be fine." He just *had* to be, Logan added silently, moving closer and putting his arms around Ali. After the past few days, she didn't deserve anything less than a perfectly happy ending.

She leaned against him, all softness and warmth. She smelled so sweet that he thought of chocolate chip cookies and forbidden desire again. The crazy combination that drove him crazy with wanting her. Her breath, warm against his neck, fanned his longing and made him want to kiss her so badly the urge was almost overwhelming. But how could he want her so incredibly much when he knew the timing was impossible?

"You know," she murmured, "it's ironic, but we were talking about depression in one of my classes not long ago. And when the instructor was trying to explain how clinically depressed people feel, she said they sometimes talk about the *black dogs.*"

Silently, Logan stroked her hair. Depression didn't strike him as the greatest topic for discussion at the moment, but if she felt like talking he wasn't going to interrupt her.

"I didn't really understand what that meant then," she went on, "but now I do. I feel as if there are black dogs and black panthers and black crocodiles, all coming after me at once. And, Logan, if Robbie doesn't make it through this all right, I'm going to die."

"I know." He continued just to stroke her hair, forcing himself to keep his other hand motionless on her back. "But Robbie's going to be fine. He'll phone in the morning and he'll be home in no time. Then we'll have him and Cody racing around here again, yelling at the top of their lungs."

"And asking for cookies."

"Yeah ... asking for cookies." Chocolate chip cookies. God, if he was going to get out of Ali's room he had to do it now, while he still thought he might be able to manage it.

"Logan?" she whispered.

"Uh-huh?"

"Would you do something for me?"

"Sure. What?"

"Would you stay here with me for a while? Just ... just be with me, I mean? I don't think I can stand to be alone right now."

"Sure ... sure I know. Why don't we turn out the light, and I'll just sit here with you."

When she gave him a wan smile, he switched off the bedside lamp, then closed his eyes and began trying to will away his aching desire.

FOR A MOMENT, Ali clung to the edge of sleep. Then the phone rang a second time and awareness flooded her. On the bedside table, the clock clicked to 2:13. Beside her in the darkness, Logan groggily muttered something. She grabbed for the phone, but she couldn't reach far enough because Logan was lying on top of the quilt, weighing it down.

When she pushed at him, her hands pressed against the soft wool of his sweater. He was still fully dressed, she realized. He'd just dozed off on the bed.

"Mmmrrrppphhh," he groaned, rolling away a little.

She tried for the phone again, reaching it this time. "Hello," she said breathlessly, getting the receiver to her ear.

"It's me," Bob said.

Her heart stopped.

"Are you there?"

"Yes! Yes, what is it?"

"What?" Logan demanded beside her.

She pressed her fingers against his lips. It made her aware her hand was trembling.

"Bob, is Robbie all right?"

"It's Bob?" Logan whispered, despite her fingers.

"Robbie's fine," Bob said. "But I want to talk to you about him."

"All right, I'm listening."

Logan switched on the bedside light and shoved himself up into a sitting position.

"I've been thinking this isn't too good for him," Bob went on. "Being away from home, I mean."

Ali closed her eyes. He was only realizing that now?

"Just a second," he said. "I'm on a car phone and I'm coming to an underpass. I'll probably lose you for a minute."

Barely breathing, she sat listening to the static grow and fade again.

"So I was thinking," Bob finally continued, "about what you said before."

"About *what* that I said?" She waited for him to continue, her heart pounding like crazy now.

"You know. You said you'd give me your word I'd get the money—even if I let Robbie come home before Friday."

Her heart stopped again. "You're saying you'll do that?" she whispered.

"I'm saying I've been thinking about it. You *did* arrange to have the money transferred?"

"Yes! Yes, of course! I did it right after you gave me the instructions. It'll be in Switzerland on Friday, be in your account for sure."

"And you wouldn't change the instructions...*if* I let Robbie go in the morning, I mean."

"No! Oh, Lord, Bob, I swear I wouldn't. I'll swear on anything you want—on Robbie's life." She waited, not breathing again, as if that could magically prevent him from saying the wrong thing.

"All right," he said at last. "Then we've got a deal. I'll set things up. Bye, Ali."

When he clicked off she simply sat holding the receiver.

"Ali?" Logan said. "Ali, you're shaking. What did he say?"

She shook her head, too filled with emotion to speak. She'd never felt this way before, but what a heavenly way to feel—as if the proverbial ten-ton weight had just been lifted off her shoulders. Fireworks were exploding all around her and the black dogs of depression were racing away into the night.

"Ali, for God's sake, what?"

Tears began streaming down her face and Logan wrapped his arms around her and pulled her to him. "Oh, God, Ali, what's happening now?"

"No, no," she managed to say, "you don't understand. He's going to let Robbie come home."

"Oh, God," Logan said again, this time in relief. He'd been thinking the worst.

"When?" he asked, taking her by the arms and gazing at her.

"He said in the morning. Just as soon as he sets it up, I guess. Oh, Logan, you've been right all along. Everything's going to be fine." Ali threw her arms around his neck and clung to him.

With her body pressed against his, he was excruciatingly aware she had on only that silky nightshirt.

"I...I don't know what made him change his mind," she murmured. "Why he decided to trust me. He said he'd been thinking this wasn't good for Robbie, but I'm sure there's more to it than that. It doesn't matter why, though. Oh, Logan, it doesn't matter why at all, does it?"

"No," he whispered into her hair. "No, it doesn't matter why."

He'd bet he knew, though. After his near miss with Nick Sinclair last night, Bob had decided the sooner he got out of Toronto the better. Maybe he'd even decided that sticking around until Friday might prove fatal. But at least the guy had turned out to have *some* sense of decency. At least he was going to make sure Robbie was safely home before he took off, not leave him with some stranger until Friday.

"Oh, Logan," Ali said against his chest. "The past few days have been so awful, but now I feel . . ."

She paused, suddenly aware of exactly how she *did* feel. She felt positively euphoric. And incredibly aroused. The horror of the past few days was almost over. Robbie would be home in the morning, and that was only a few hours away. She'd been so, so afraid, but one phone call was all it had taken to dissipate her fear.

That had allowed room for other emotions to surface, and now that they had . . . well, Logan Reed was definitely a man she felt other emotions for. There was no point in going back to her silly game of denying it. The way she felt about him . . .

It was impossible to put into words, but if he hadn't been here for her, she wouldn't have made it through this. It was as simple as that. The black dogs would have dragged her down and the black crocodiles would have swallowed her up. She shifted a little in his arms, so she could see his face. Just looking at it made her smile.

"What?" he asked, giving her an uncertain smile in return.

He had an absolutely gorgeous face—all those chiseled planes and angles. And she loved the blue of his eyes. They were such a deep ocean blue she could almost drown in his gaze. And, right now, he had the most enticing four o'clock shadow she'd ever seen.

Reaching up, she trailed her fingers slowly along his jaw, rough with stubble . . . then across his lips, so full and sensuous that just touching them started her fantasies simmering. Had it been only a day ago that he'd held her in his arms and kissed her? It seemed as if the memory of his kisses had been lingering in her mind for a long, long time.

Finally, he gently brushed *his* fingers across *her* lips. His touch sent a hot little rush through her, and she rested her hand on his chest.

"You fell asleep with your clothes on," she murmured, smoothing a path across his sweater.

He trapped her hand with his, then just sat looking at her.

She smiled at him once more, realizing these were the first smiles that had felt real since Robbie had disappeared.

"They get crumpled," she finally said when he didn't seem to be catching her drift. "Your clothes . . . when you sleep in them they get crumpled. So you should take them off."

"I should, eh?" He gave her a grin, but didn't move.

"Definitely."

"You sure, Ali?" he said quietly, his grin fading. "You've been in pretty rough shape, so you're sure you'd feel okay about that?"

"I'm sure I'd feel wonderful about it," she murmured, leaning closer to kiss him.

Chapter Twelve

The kiss was hot and hungry, igniting a fire deep inside her. Not a simmering fantasy fire, but a molten sexual reality that turned her liquid with desire.

"Oh, God," Logan murmured at last. "I've thought about this for so long, Ali. I've wanted you so badly that I had to pretend I didn't really care at all, just to keep hold of my sanity around you."

"You, too?" she whispered.

That made him laugh out loud. Then, tugging his sweater off, he stood and quickly removed the rest of his clothes.

He turned and gazed at her, and she drank in his gorgeous nakedness like a woman dying of thirst. Which she was, really, because it had been so long.

Far too long. Yet until now, until Logan, she hadn't realized that—hadn't felt any desire. But he made her feel as if she wouldn't be complete until they'd made love. He was all raw, real male, with hard muscles begging to be touched and hard arousal begging to be taken inside her.

"What about this?" He leaned forward and rested his fingers against her throat, just below the top of her

nightshirt. Then he slid them slowly along its neck-
line, the backs of his fingers brushing her skin. It
burned beneath his touch, and a fresh rush of fire
raced through her veins.

"It would be in the way," she murmured, raising
her arms to let him pull the shirt over her head.

When he sank back onto the bed she wrapped her
arms around his neck, already wanting him so desperately she ached.

He pulled her down beside him, cradling her face
between his hands and covering her mouth greedily
with his. He kissed her lips, her eyes, her throat—
found the pulse just above her collarbone and started
it racing with his tongue.

She tangled her fingers in his hair, then ran her
hands down his back, loving the feel of his body.

Moaning when his fingers moved lightly to her
breasts, she pressed herself against him as he began to
caress her nipples. His body, touching hers, stoked the
fire within her, making it hotter yet, while his clever
mouth and hands made the flames dance.

"Oh, Logan," she murmured, "hurry, I can't
wait."

"Sure you can," he whispered, his mouth so close
to her breast that she could feel the warmth of his
breath. It sent a ripple of unadulterated need through
her.

"After all this time, you can wait a little longer,
Ali."

But when his mouth closed over her nipple and he
began to tease it with his tongue, she couldn't wait
another second. Stronger ripples surged through her,

coming so quickly, one after another, that they made her moan and whimper and cry his name. Fire sparked everywhere within her, her heartbeat was thunder in her ears, breathing became all but impossible.

Then, just when she knew she was about to die, a final wave of heat rushed through her, leaving shimmering relief in its wake. She couldn't move, could only gasp for breath, could only whisper unintelligible murmurs of love. And then he moved his hand lower and began to stoke the fire again, bringing her to the edge of madness with his touch.

"Logan," she whispered desperately. "Logan, please."

At last he covered her with his body and buried himself in her. She locked her legs around him and clung to him, each deep thrust sending her to the brink, each stroke back leaving her weak and senseless.

Her body arched against his, seeking release again. And suddenly his control was gone, taking the shreds that remained of hers with it.

She was lost in a blinding explosion of dark heat that carried them both over the edge—into an electric rush of free-fall. Then, as their fall gradually slowed, as the shudders within them began to still, Logan sagged against her.

She drank in his weight, his earthy male scent, the ragged sound of his breathing. Their bodies were slick with love, and the scent of it hung in the air around them. The scent of love. She was in love with Logan Reed. The realization had just kind of snuck up on her over the past few days. But now that it had, simply thinking about it made her smile.

He curled onto his side, pulling her so close her breasts were pressed against his chest. She rested her head in the pillow of his shoulder and lay dreamily in his arms. "Why did we wait so long?" she finally whispered.

He kissed the tip of her nose. "Because I didn't think you wanted me. Because I was pretending I didn't want you. Because I kept refusing to admit you're the most beautiful woman I've ever met."

"I'm not," she said, delighted that he thought she was.

He propped himself up on his elbow and gazed at her in the dim light of the bedside lamp. "Let's see . . . gorgeous coppery gold hair."

Pausing, he brushed a few strands of it gently back from her face. "Strawberry blond . . . that's what it's called, right? Plus big brown eyes, long lashes and skin like silk." He ran his fingers down her nakedness, making her tremble. "Not to even mention those sexy bunny slippers you wear. And a mouth . . ."

He leaned closer and gave her a deep, drugging kiss. Impossible as it seemed, that started a new throbbing of need within her.

"Nah," he whispered, snuggling back down beside her. "Nothing beautiful about you at all. Nothing a man would ever even think about falling in love with."

"Not a man like you, at least," she murmured, trying her hardest to sound as if she was teasing, not fishing.

"Oh, I don't know about that, Ali. You aren't counting on it, are you?"

She tangled her fingers in his chest hair, not wanting to meet his gaze because he'd be certain to see the truth in her eyes.

"Hey," he finally said, tucking his fingers under her chin and forcing her to look at him. "I don't want to play this game anymore. I think we've been playing it for longer than either of us want to admit and...well, I love you, Ali. So how does that strike you?"

She tried not to smile but couldn't help it. "It strikes me as fair enough. Perfectly fair, in fact, considering the way I feel about you."

ALI WOKE UP feeling so euphoric she was certain she was still dreaming. Then she cuddled against the warmth of Logan's body and knew she wasn't. No dream could possibly make her feel *that* good.

The bedroom was still dark. Not even the palest fingers of dawn had begun to creep through the crack between the bedroom curtains. But daybreak came late at the end of the year, and the bedside clock told her it was morning.

The morning. The morning Robbie was coming home. Thinking about that made her happier still, and she couldn't resist kissing Logan. "Good morning," she whispered when he stirred.

"Mmmrrrppphhh," he mumbled, wrapping his arms around her and taking charge of the kiss.

"God," he finally murmured. "You beat the hell out of an alarm clock. You think you could wake me up like that every morning?"

She snuggled as closely as she could to him, feeling so warm in the shelter of his arms, so protected from the outside world, from any thoughts she didn't want intruding. And then some of them insisted on forcing their way in, reminding her that *every* morning wasn't a possibility. Not a very long-term one, at least.

They, Logan had told her, wanted him in L.A. by the end of January. And today, assuming her brain was working right, was the twenty-first of December. She pulled the quilt more tightly over her, hating the anonymous *they.* She wasn't so protected from the outside world after all. Its cold chill had just reached right into her bed.

"What are you thinking about?" Logan asked, trailing his fingers down her arm.

"The truth?"

When he nodded, she simply continued to gaze at him. He was utterly gorgeous, but she loved him for far more than his looks. She loved how solid and steady he was, loved that she knew she could rely on him. But that would only be the case for such a short while longer.

"Aren't you going to tell me?" he asked.

She hesitated for another moment, then said, "I was thinking about Robbie coming home today and about you leaving."

"Leaving?"

"For California."

"Oh...yeah. I've been forgetting all about that the past few days."

She waited, but he didn't go on. Didn't say the words she wanted to hear—that he was having second thoughts about being so far away from her, that the way things had changed between them made an important difference.

And when he finally did speak, he still didn't say the right words.

"I *have* to go, you know," he said quietly. "My agent went through hell to convince the producers I could do the job, and it's the chance of a lifetime."

"I know."

"If I didn't show up, I'd be blowing any hopes of a career in the film industry. Instead of maybe being rich and famous, my name would be mud."

"I know," she murmured again, hating his agent— the faceless Connie, who'd worked so hard to get him his chance to do that screen adaptation. Would it have hurt her to have worked just a little less hard?

Ali stared at one of the swirls of hair on Logan's chest, knowing she was being utterly selfish. Just as he'd said, this was the chance of a lifetime. So had she really thought he'd consider throwing it away because the neighbor lady had let herself fall in love with him? *Foolishly* let herself, knowing all along there was no future for them?

Come the new year, she'd go back to her classes and Logan would go to L.A. And, in no time flat, those Hollywood starlets would make him forget all about the neighbor lady.

"Hey," he said, pulling her close again, "I love you, Ali. And you love me, right? You haven't changed your mind since last night, have you?"

She shook her head against his shoulder, breathing in the masculine scent that was uniquely his.

"Good, then as long as that's the case, we'll work something out. Hell, maybe I'll be a total failure as a scriptwriter, and they'll ship me back here in only a week or two. If it turns out I'm going to be gone for a long time, though—"

"Or forever," she murmured.

"Or forever," he repeated quietly. "But how long isn't the point. The point is that I don't want to lose you. You believe that, don't you?"

"Yes," she whispered. But it was one thing believing when he was here in her bed, with his arms securely around her. It would be another thing entirely when he was gone.

"Good. So we'll work things out somehow. Right?"

"Right."

Logan tilted her face to his and kissed her.

It was a long, loving kiss full of promises. But she couldn't help wondering if there was any chance those promises would become reality. Couldn't help thinking about the old song that said absence makes the heart grow fonder—for somebody else.

"SITTING THERE staring at it won't make it ring, you know," Logan said gently.

Ali glanced over to where he was leaning against the kitchen counter and shrugged.

"Hey, try to stop worrying. It's only ten after nine, and Bob didn't say exactly when he'd call, did he."

She shook her head. In fact, he hadn't specifically told her he'd call at all.

"I'll set things up" was what he'd said. So maybe he'd just have somebody drop Robbie off.

Resisting the urge to run to the front of the house and check the street, she sat right where she was and concentrated on trying to ignore the anxiety gnawing away at her. Then she looked at the phone again and the gnawing grew worse.

After Logan had talked to his parents and Cody this morning, he'd connected the tape recorder once more. She hadn't asked him why, though, because she knew she wouldn't like the answer. Despite his nonchalant act, why would Logan care whether he could replay this call—assuming there was going to be one—unless he thought something still might go wrong?

She was trying to force that question from her mind when the phone rang. The recorder's light flashed on. Across the room Logan tensed, his nonchalant act clearly forgotten.

Ali took a deep breath, picked up the receiver and said, "Hello."

"Hello," a woman replied. "Is this Ali Weyden?"

"Yes." Her heart was hammering in anticipation. Did the call have something to do with Robbie or not?

"I have a message for you, Mrs. Weyden. From your husband."

Oh, Lord, this was it. "Yes?" she managed to say again.

There was a slight pause, a few rustling, whispering noises in the background, then the woman went on. "The message is that your package is waiting for you, and you should go pick it up at Mr. Velarde's cottage."

The line clicked dead. It was over. She knew where Robbie was. She felt both weak with relief and numb with shock.

"It was Vinny," she whispered. "He was the one helping Bob after all."

"What?" Logan demanded. "What's the deal?" He pushed the rewind switch, then played back the tape.

"At *Vinny's* cottage?" he snarled, hearing the message. "That's where they've had Robbie? That lying bastard! Dammit, Ali, I'm going to kill him. I swear, I'll go back down to his office and kill him with my bare hands."

Ali sat gazing across the table, not knowing whether to laugh or cry. She was too happy about Robbie to be as angry as Logan seemed. That would come, she was sure, but she could handle only so much emotion at once. And right now, knowing where her son was seemed like all that was important.

"Could we go get Robbie first?" she said at last. "Could you wait and kill Vinny later?"

The muscles in Logan's jaw relaxed and he grinned at her. "Yeah, yeah, I guess we'd better keep our priorities straight."

He strode around the table, pulled her up out of her chair and swung her around in his arms. "We did it, Ali," he murmured against her throat. "We did it. Robbie's almost home."

He gave her a quick kiss, then said, "I guess we'd better save any serious kissing for later and get going. You know exactly where Vinny's cottage is?"

She nodded. "Bob and I used to go up there for the odd weekend, years ago."

"How far? How long will it take us?"

"A couple of hours. Maybe just a little longer. It's on Lake Muskoka."

A couple of hours. The phrase began merrily playing in her mind. In hardly no time at all, she'd have Robbie back. She felt like hugging herself and dancing in the street—both at once.

"We'll take the Jeep," Logan said, grabbing Ali's hand and starting for the front hall. "The roads up there might not be very well plowed." He shrugged into his jacket, then waited impatiently, with the door open, while she tugged on her boots. "The voice," he said as she locked the door behind them. "The woman who phoned. I guess you'd have said something if her voice had sounded familiar."

She nodded. "It didn't. Not at all. You think it was the woman who's been looking after Robbie?"

"Could be. She could easily have been calling from Muskoka."

As they headed through the cold morning air, down Ali's driveway and along the street to Logan's, he was already thinking about which route would get them up to Muskoka fastest. He wanted to reach Vinny's cottage as quickly as possible. Because he couldn't put his finger on exactly what it was, but *something* was bothering him about that phone call.

Then, suddenly, he had something else to worry about. Just as they were about to get into the Cherokee, Nick Sinclair's black Caddy rolled along the street. It slowed almost to a stop as it passed his driveway, then continued on toward College.

"Hurry up," he said, practically pushing Ali into the Jeep. "I just want to get going," he added, when she looked at him strangely.

He quickly climbed in the driver's side and started the engine. She hadn't noticed the Caddy and he sure as hell didn't intend to tell her it had been by. But he'd obviously been too quick in thinking the guy was through staking out her house. Or maybe he'd been coming by to have another talk with her.

Whichever it was, in case Sinclair decided to follow them, he wanted to be out of sight and halfway to the Parkway before that Caddy had a chance to turn around.

SNOW-COVERED FIELDS stretched along both sides of Highway 11, but the pavement was clear and they'd made good time—had almost reached Gravenhurst, at the southern tip of Lake Muskoka. So far, so good, Logan was thinking. If Sinclair *had* tried to tail them, he'd blown it. There'd been no sign at all of the Caddy.

"It's really a winter wonderland up here, isn't it," Ali murmured. "Look at the sun on all that snow. You know, we should take the boys someplace like this next week and do a little cross-country."

"Good idea," he said, glancing over at her, then ahead at the road again.

Yesterday, he knew she wouldn't have noticed a single thing about the surroundings. And she sure wouldn't have been making plans for an outing with

Robbie and Cody. That phone call had made a world of difference in her. She even *looked* more relaxed. There was still something nagging at him about it, though, and he wished to hell he could figure out what.

"You sure that woman's voice didn't sound even a little familiar?" he asked.

She smiled. "You think I'll magically realize it did— if you keep asking me about it every twenty minutes?"

"Well...I keep wondering if she was disguising it. What about Vinny's wife? It sound anything like her?"

"Mimi? No. Besides, she's away. Vinny said she was at a spa someplace, remember?"

"Yeah, well, we can't exactly rely on anything *Vinny* said, can we. Hell, for all we know, it's his wife who's been taking care of Robbie."

Ali smiled again and shook her head. "Mimi would never let herself get stuck in a cottage with a six-year-old. She hates kids, so it would be totally out of character. After I had Robbie, she never invited Bob and me up here again. Go right, up ahead there," she added after a minute. "You want Muskoka Road 17."

Logan eased up on the gas.

"It's not too far now," Ali told him once they'd left the main highway behind.

Excitement was audible in her voice, and Logan reached over and squeezed her hand. Then he made himself concentrate on his driving. The secondary road was covered in packed snow, and there were probably icy patches. The last thing they needed was to find themselves in the ditch.

"Turn at that little intersection coming up," Ali said.

He turned and they were on a narrow back road. Only a single lane had been plowed, and it wasn't much wider than the Jeep. If he met a car coming the other way, one of them would be doing a lot of backing up. He was still half thinking about that when something Ali had said struck him. She knew it wouldn't be Vinny's wife who was taking care of Robbie because it would be totally out of character.

Out of character... that was it! That's what had been bothering him.

If that phone call this morning had been in a novel, in one of *his* novels, at least, it would have been *Bob* who'd phoned. He'd made all the previous calls himself, so having someone else call Ali today had been out of character. But was there any *significance* to that, or was wondering about it just an example of his writer's imagination working overtime?

"There it is," Ali said. "See that wooden sign ahead? That's their place."

The sign she was pointing to was a cedar one that read Velarde's Hideout, and the narrow drive it marked had fresh tire tracks in the recent dusting of snow.

Logan turned in, his adrenaline pumping and his brain clicking over. *Velarde's Hideout.* What kind of guy would name his cottage that? One who figured he was a throwback to Jesse James or somebody?

The idea of an outlaw's hideout started him think-ing about Vinny's damned innocent routine again. What a crock that had been, right from the word go— from claiming he didn't know anything about what had happened to Robbie, to saying he'd never known Bob was into smuggling for the mob. Vinny was probably just as much of a criminal as Bob had ever been.

And wasn't that just terrific. Those two were the ones calling the shots, and odds were that neither of them could be trusted an inch. Logan glanced at Ali again, praying that Bob and Vinny could at least be trusted when it came to Robbie. Then the drive curved and Velarde's Hideout was visible ahead of them.

Logan stopped the Jeep and sat scoping out the scene. The cottage, set in a clearing surrounded by trees and bush, was an expensive-looking log A-frame—a modified design with one side extending out a good fifteen feet more than the other. The longer side had a large window in it, so that was likely the living room.

There was nobody in sight, but from the looks of things somebody was definitely waiting for them. There was a late-model BMW parked at the end of the drive and smoke was lazily drifting from the chim-ney.

"Recognize the car?" he asked Ali.

She hesitated. "No, not that specific one, but Mimi always drove a Bimmer. So, while she's away, Vinny could have been letting . . . whoever use it."

Logan nodded. The unknown *whoever*. Maybe that was his problem, maybe it was not knowing exactly what they were walking into that was making him uneasy. Somebody was in that cottage with Robbie, but it wasn't necessarily the woman who'd phoned... wasn't necessarily a woman at all. It could be Vinny. Hell, it could even be Bob.

For the second time in the past few days he wished he had a gun. Apparently, there was nothing like getting involved with the criminal element to make you wish you had something that would even things up a little. Reminding himself they'd been *told* to come here, that they wouldn't be taking anybody by surprise, he reached for the driver's door handle.

"No, you stay here," he told Ali when she reached for hers.

She gave him a look that said he'd lost his mind if he thought she would, and opened her door.

Swearing silently, Logan climbed out his side. If anything unexpected happened, he'd far rather have her back in the car than right beside him.

"I don't see Robbie," she said as they hurried along the drive. "I thought he'd be watching out the window for me."

Her stomach full of butterflies, she raced up the steps ahead of Logan and knocked. Then she waited, heart pounding. Any second now, the door would fly open and Robbie would throw himself at her. But the door didn't open. And she couldn't hear any sound from inside. She glanced anxiously at Logan.

He knocked, far more insistently than she had.

When there was still no answer, the butterflies began to multiply rapidly. Where was her son?

"Wait here," Logan said, turning and starting back down the steps.

Ali stood watching him, shivering a little, her breath visible in the air.

It was even colder up here than it had been in the city. She'd guess at least twenty below. And when Logan headed across the front of the cottage, toward the living room window, the snow was well over the tops of his cowboy boots. She could practically feel the wet iciness seeping through the legs of his jeans, but he kept plowing doggedly ahead until he reached the window.

He peered in for a couple of seconds, rapped loudly on the glass, then started back through the snow. "There's someone in there," he muttered when he reached the door again. "I think it was a woman but it was hard to tell. She was all bundled up in a quilt or something. And either she's hard-of-hearing or she was ignoring us."

"She's coming now, though?"

"Yeah, it's tougher to ignore a face at your window than a knock on your door."

"But you didn't see Robbie?"

"No, I guess he must be—"

The door flew open, but Robbie wasn't there to throw himself at Ali.

Instead, Mimi Velarde stood glaring at them, a scarf wrapped around her head, hiding most her face.

"Mimi," Ali whispered, not certain whether she was more taken aback by what little she could see of Mimi's face or by the gun she was pointing at them.

Chapter Thirteen

Logan's shocked gaze was locked on the pistol. He'd never before had a woman answer a door aiming a semiautomatic at his chest. Hell, he'd never before had *anyone* do it. *Mimi,* Ali had called her. Which meant she was Vinny's wife, even though Ali had been sure she wouldn't be the one with Robbie. When the woman slowly lowered the pistol, he followed it with his eyes—just to make sure it ended up pointed safely at the ground.

"Sorry," she was saying, "I didn't know who was out here and . . . but what a surprise you are, Ali."

Why, Logan wondered, was Mimi surprised? Hadn't anyone told her they were coming? He forced his eyes from the gun and up to Mimi's face, hoping to see some answers written on it.

Instead of answers he got another shock. Behind that scarf, Mimi's face was almost as bruised as Vinny's had been the other day. Her bruises weren't nearly as fresh, though. In fact, they were well on their way to disappearing. But her skin was still tinged with purple and blue, and liberally spotted with large patches of yellow.

Fleetingly, he thought that Vinny might not have had a run-in with Nick Sinclair's muscle at all. Maybe the truth was that Vinny and Mimi were just into real rough stuff. Or maybe Mimi'd had a run-in with Nick Sinclair's muscle, too. At this point, Logan wouldn't rule anything out as being beyond belief.

"I came for Robbie," Ali was saying uncertainly. Seeing Mimi's face had obviously thrown her, as well.

"Robbie?" Mimi repeated. "You mean your Robbie? What on earth would he be doing here?"

Ali shot Logan a look of total panic and he wrapped his arm securely around her shoulders.

"Robbie's not here?" he asked Mimi. "You haven't seen him?"

"I haven't seen him since he was two years old," she snapped. "And who are you?"

"I'm a friend of Ali's. And we were told Robbie was here."

"Well, he isn't. Why on earth would somebody... who said he was?"

"Mrs. Velarde," Logan said quietly, "Robbie was kidnapped a few days ago."

The anger disappeared from Mimi's expression, leaving only confusion. "Kidnapped?" she repeated. "And someone said he was *here?*"

Logan nodded.

"My God... Oh, Ali, I'm sorry. This is the first I've heard about it. But please, come in," she added, taking Ali's arm. "Come and sit down. Tell me what's happened."

It took Logan all of two seconds to realize that Bob's throwing them a curve had catapulted Ali into the depths of despair. So, when they sat down, *he* filled Mimi in on the basics of what had been going on.

"And that's about it," he said, reaching the end. He leaned back beside Ali, trying to read Mimi's reactions. Thus far, he hadn't been able to decide whether this was really the first she'd heard of Robbie's disappearance or not. She was sitting on the other side of the fireplace from them, on the couch facing theirs— her scarf discarded, her discolored face no longer concealed.

The cause of her bruises had turned out to be far more mundane than he'd speculated. She'd simply had a face-lift and was hiding out while the scars healed. The bit about going to a spa had been a cover.

She *had* been out of town for a couple of weeks, though—seeing Vinny only when he came to the cottage on the weekends. So possibly she really hadn't known anything. On the other hand, she might just be *playing* innocent.

"Sunday," she finally murmured. "You said this happened Sunday. You mean, while Vinny and I were sitting here in front of the fire, poor little Robbie..."

Had Vinny been sitting here, though? Logan wondered. Or had he been the one behind those panels in the clinic, waiting to grab his partner's son.

"But why," Mimi went on, "would that woman tell you Robbie was *here?*"

"We have no idea. And now that we know he isn't..." Logan covered Ali's hand with his. Now they were back to square one.

"This is unbelievable," Mimi said. "I mean, *the whole thing* is unbelievable—Bob not really being dead, taking Robbie. My God, Ali, you must be absolutely frantic, but I'm sure everything will turn out fine. I mean, as awful as it is for you, you know Bob would take good care of his own son. I mean . . . he *would,* wouldn't he?"

"We're counting on that," Logan said. He only wished he believed they *could* count on it.

"So it's going to be fine in the end. But it's all so . . . well, I know I'm being repetitious, but unbelievable is the only word. Vinny must have been shocked out of his mind when you told him. But why on earth didn't he tell me? He phones every night."

Neither Logan nor Ali offered a possible explanation for that, so Mimi came up with one of her own. "I guess he didn't want me worrying about Robbie. That must have been it."

"Mmm," Logan said noncommittally. He was certain that wasn't it at all, but damned if he had a clue what the real reason might be—assuming Mimi *had* been in the dark until now.

"Yes, that must have been it," she said again. "The doctor warned me to avoid stress while I was recovering from the surgery, so I guess Vinny was thinking about that.

"But what I *really* can't figure out is that phone call. You said the woman told you her message was from Bob?"

When Logan nodded, Mimi pushed herself up from the couch and paced across the room. She stopped in front of a desk in the corner and stood drumming her fingernails on it. "Why on earth," she asked at last, "would Bob have wanted you to come *here?*"

"Well...we assumed Vinny had offered Bob the use of the cottage."

"What?" Mimi said incredulously. "You mean you thought Vinny *knew* what Bob was up to?"

Logan shrugged. "We figured Bob might have asked him for help. After all, they were partners for a long time," he added, trying not to sound as if he was blaming Vinny. It wouldn't get them anywhere to say they'd suspected her husband had been in on things all along.

"Oh, no," she was saying firmly. "Oh, no, I don't know what's going on any more than you do, but Vinny would never be part of something like this. Besides, *I've* been up here for two weeks. So this is the last place Vinny would have suggested—*if* he'd wanted to help Bob, which I know he wouldn't have."

As she finished speaking, Mimi glanced into the mirror hanging behind the desk and muttered something to herself. Then she looked back across the room, saying, "God, what a wreck I am, eh? I was supposed to have recovered entirely in a couple of weeks, but I turned out to be a slow healer. And now I've had to cancel out on a bunch of Christmas parties.

"Oh...sorry, that was an awfully insensitive thing to say, wasn't it, Ali. But when I saw myself in the mirror...you've got this trouble, though, and my problems are the last thing you want to hear about. So, look, tell me what I can do to help. Do you want me to phone Vinny? Right now? He's out of the office a lot, so I can't always reach him during the day, but I can try—just make *certain* he hasn't heard anything from Bob."

"No," Logan said. "No, I'm sure you're right. Vinny doesn't know anything." Actually, the only thing he was sure of was that Mimi's phoning would get them nowhere. If she did reach Vinny, he'd say whatever suited him.

"Well, look, take the number here. In case you change your minds or anything. If you want me to try to get him before tonight, I will." She rummaged in the desk for a piece of paper, scribbled the number on it and handed it to Logan.

"Bob's sending you up here, though... that's still what I can't figure out. It just doesn't make any sense, does it. I mean, it was nothing but a wild-goose chase."

Suddenly, Logan felt like a prize idiot. Why hadn't that occurred to him right off the bat?

He turned to Ali, saying, "Bob wanted you out of the house. *That's* why we're here. Because he wanted to make sure you'd be gone for a few hours."

"But why?" she whispered.

Logan sat rubbing his jaw. Damned if he knew. But he'd bet they were going to find out when they got home.

ALI CLASPED HER HANDS tightly in her lap as Logan turned off Bloor and started down Palmerston. She'd spent the entire drive back wishing they could get home faster. But now that they were almost there, she was scared to death about what they'd find. Or, to be accurate, about what they wouldn't find.

They'd only managed to come up with one possible explanation for Bob's having sent them on what had been, as Mimi had so rightly called it, a wild-goose chase. The single reason that seemed logical was that he'd arranged for someone to drop Robbie safely off at home and had wanted her out of the house so she wouldn't see anything she could tell the police later. She'd been trying not even to let herself hope that was it, though, because she didn't know what she'd do if Robbie *wasn't* there waiting for her.

Logan stopped at the intersection of Harbord, then proceeded across. She still couldn't see the house, but in only another block—

"Dammit to hell," he muttered, sharply hitting the brakes.

Her eyes flashed to him.

He was staring straight ahead, and when her gaze followed his her heart began to pound.

Nick Sinclair was casually standing in their path. His coat was open to the cold and he'd obviously just stepped out of the Caddy. It was tucked in between two other parked cars, the driver's door wide open.

"That's Sinclair?" Logan asked.

She nodded, too frightened to speak. *Now* what was happening?

"I'll talk to him," Logan said, reaching for the door handle. "You stay where you are."

"No! You stay here with me! I'm the one he wants to talk to."

Logan muttered something under his breath, but sat where he was while Nick Sinclair sauntered over to her side of the Jeep.

When he tapped on the window she opened it, her hand trembling.

"What do you want?" Logan demanded, leaning halfway across her.

"You've been gone a long time, Mrs. Weyden," Sinclair said, ignoring both Logan and his question. "We've been waiting to talk to you about something."

Ali glanced anxiously at the Caddy again, expecting the human gorilla to have materialized from inside.

"Nah, I'm on my own," Sinclair said. "Gonzalez is parked down on College. We didn't know which way you'd be coming and we wanted to talk to you before you got home. You might have some people dropping by who I don't wanna run into."

She shook her head, not understanding what he was talking about. He'd definitely been waiting for her, though. That much was clear. "You wanted to talk to me about what?" she finally managed.

"About your kid."

"Oh, my Lord," she whispered.

"Hey, don't go getting hysterical on me, huh? The kid's fine. I just wanna help you make sure he stays that way."

"Get to the point," Logan snapped. "You know where Robbie is?"

Sinclair shrugged. "That's *not* the point. The point is, your friend here might have some visitors, and if she does, I wanna make sure she doesn't say anything to them about me."

"What visitors?" Ali managed to ask.

"You'll see. They might ask you some questions. And I don't want you bringing my name into the conversation. I've never been to your house. You've never met me. If they happen to ask about me, you've never even heard of me. You understand what I'm saying?"

"Yes. Yes, I understand. But what about Robbie?"

"I told you, he's fine. And he stays fine as long as you do like I say. So... you still getting that two million on Friday?"

She nodded, not knowing whether that was the right or wrong thing to do.

"And Bob tell you where to meet him with it yet?"

"No... no, not yet."

"Ahh. Well, if you don't hear from him about it, you'll hear from me. You don't really care *who* you give that money to, do you? Not so long as you get the kid back safe, right? And by the way, don't say anything about *him* to your visitors, neither. About him not being around right now, I mean. You do that, and he won't be around permanently... you understand what I'm saying?"

Behind them, a driver unable to get past the Cherokee tooted his horn. Sinclair glanced in the man's direction and gave him a finger. Then, without another word, he turned and started back toward the Caddy.

"He's got Robbie," Ali whispered. "My God, Logan, *he's* got Robbie."

"No, he doesn't," Logan said, even though he didn't have any idea who had what. "Just let me get out of the way here," he added, driving forward, past Sinclair's car, then pulling in across the entrance to a driveway.

The car they'd been blocking drove past. In the rearview mirror, he could see Sinclair backing up the Caddy. Then he swung it out onto Harbord and was gone. But that probably wasn't the last they'd see of him, which was far from the most reassuring thought in the world.

Ali had started trembling and tears were trickling down her cheeks, so Logan pulled her close and held her. "Listen to me," he murmured, thinking fast and trying to add up everything they knew.

"Sinclair *doesn't* have Robbie," he finally said more firmly, deciding that had to be true. "If he did, why wouldn't he have come right out and said so? And remember when he showed up at your door on Monday? You told me he said he didn't know where Robbie was. All he knew was that Bob had him. And he only knew that because they'd bugged your phone, remember?"

"But..." Ali didn't go on, simply gazed tearfully at him.

"Look, he just wants you to *think* he has Robbie. So you won't say anything to...to whoever he figures is going to come around asking questions."

"I won't. I can't take the chance that maybe...I just can't take *any* chances."

Logan nodded. As much as he hated the idea of her lying to protect a creep like Sinclair, he knew she'd do anything to help keep Robbie safe. Even if there was only a chance in a million it actually would.

"But, Logan," she whispered, "do you know what's going on? Do you understand all this any better than I do? *Who* doesn't he want me to say anything to? And what did he mean about the money? That bit about maybe hearing from him about it, instead of from Bob? Why would I give it to *him?* And even if that made any sense, I won't have it to give him."

"Shhh," Logan murmured, pulling her closer once more.

"And what about Robbie?" she went on, her cheek pressed against his chest. "He's not going to be waiting at home for us after all. Nobody would have gotten him there with those two goons guarding the street. Oh, Logan, this is all so crazy I can't stand it. We're never going to get Robbie back. I'm never going to see him again."

"Shhh," he murmured again. "Let's get home and we'll talk about it then, okay?"

When she simply made a little whimpering noise in her throat he sat stroking her hair and held her while she cried.

They could drive the final block once she'd calmed down a little. By then, with any luck, he might even come up with some answers to her questions. Some answers she'd want to hear, that was.

He mentally reviewed what Sinclair had said. It *had* sounded as if he was figuring he could somehow get the two million bucks from Ali. But, as she'd said, she wasn't going to have it. All she'd have would be a brokerage receipt for its transfer to Switzerland. So if Sinclair had decided he wanted that money, and then he discovered Ali had lied to him . . .

Logan kissed the top of her head, his throat tight with fear. Last night, she'd said that if Robbie didn't make it through this she was going to die. And he knew exactly how she felt. If *she* didn't make it through this, *he* was going to die.

ALI'S HOUSE WAS EMPTY when they finally got there. No Robbie and no visitors. It wasn't long, though, before the visitors arrived.

Ali had managed to calm down somewhat, and had gone upstairs to wash her face. Logan was on his way to the kitchen to make some coffee. But as he was heading down the hall someone knocked on the front door. He swung around to face two serious-looking men standing on the porch. One was a swarthy, dark-haired guy in his late thirties, the other was balding and a little older. Both were wearing suits and overcoats. Both looked in good shape, but somewhat worn around the edges.

Logan had already guessed they were cops by the time the older one held a detective's shield up to the glass and said, "Police." He started for the door, not really surprised this was who Sinclair was worried about Ali talking to. It made the thought of her lying for him even less palatable, but what alternative did she have?

None, he thought, silently answering his own question. Because she was right. They just couldn't take any chances.

When he opened the door, the younger detective asked if Mrs. Weyden was home. Logan said she was, motioned them inside and turned to call Ali, but she was already coming down the stairs. She was still wearing the jeans and blue ski sweater she'd worn up to the cottage, but she'd put on fresh makeup. It didn't help. She looked so damned drawn and pale that he knew she couldn't take much more.

"Mrs. Weyden?" the older detective asked when she reached the bottom of the stairs.

She nodded.

"I'm Detective Frank Hallop. This is my partner, Detective Lou Mitropoulos. We'd like to talk to you for a few minutes. In there be okay?" he added, gesturing toward the living room doorway.

She simply nodded again, and they all trooped in. Hallop and Mitropoulos shrugged out of their coats, then sat down on the couch, facing the fireplace and Christmas tree. Ali took one of the wing chairs. That left Logan only the other chair, at the far end of the coffee table from her, or the love seat, way back by the window. He casually wandered over and just stood behind her chair.

"And you are . . . ?" Hallop said, eyeing him.

"My name's Logan Reed. I live a couple of doors down the street."

"Whatever you're here about," Ali said quietly, "I'd like Logan to stay."

"You a lawyer, Mr. Reed?" Mitropoulos asked.

"No. Just a friend."

Mitropoulos glanced at Hallop. When Hallop shrugged, the younger man produced a pen and notebook from his coat pocket.

"Does she *need* a lawyer?" Logan asked while Mitropoulos flipped through his book, looking for whatever page he wanted.

"No, I can't imagine why she would," Hallop said. He leaned forward, clasping his hands between his knees, and looked directly at Ali. "Mrs. Weyden, I'm afraid this is going to come as a shock to you, but your husband's body was discovered earlier today. He was murdered sometime during the night."

Chapter Fourteen

"Murdered?" Ali whispered.

"I'm afraid so," Hallop said.

Logan rested his hands on her shoulders, trying to will her strength. The pieces had suddenly fallen into place. A few of them, at any rate. Sometime after Bob had phoned in the middle of the night, Sinclair had succeeded in catching up with him. And that was why Sinclair didn't want Ali telling anyone what she knew.

But if Bob was dead, what about Robbie? That question started Logan's gut clenching. Could Sinclair really have him? Surely it wasn't possible Robbie had been with Bob last night, that when Sinclair had caught up with him . . .

Of course it was. In this crazy situation anything was possible. And he knew it was the first thing Ali would think about. He began trying to massage the back of her neck, but her muscles were so tense they felt like steel.

"Murdered," she whispered again.

This time, Hallop simply nodded, then said, "I understand you believed he'd died about eighteen months ago?"

"You're *certain* it was Bob Weyden's body?" Logan asked, trying to buy her time.

Mitropoulos nodded. "His prints are on file. The RCMP had some interest in his activities a few years back."

"Now," Hallop said, his attention focused on Ali again, "I'd like to ask you a couple of questions. First, there's been no response at Mrs. Weyden's residence. The deceased's mother, I'm referring to. Do you know if she's in town?"

"Celeste," Ali murmured. "Oh, Lord, poor Celeste."

"Is she in town?" Hallop asked a second time.

Ali nodded. "As far as I know. But when she hears about this she'll be so... She has a friend. Next door. A Margie someone. When you tell her, could you have Margie there with her?"

"We can try to arrange that," Hallop said. "And we've also gotten no one at Custom Cargoes. Only an answering machine. Would you know if Mr. Velarde is away?"

"No...no. He...I guess he just wasn't in the office."

"Fine. That helps us. Now, Mrs. Weyden, we're not treating your husband's death as a random killing, but we don't have much to go on yet. Not as far as motive was concerned. Mr. Weyden was carrying a key, though. There was no ID on the body, but there was a safety deposit key with the number 3374 on it. Does that mean anything to you?"

"No. Nothing."

"Mrs. Weyden was separated from her husband," Logan said. "The marriage had ended before he was reported dead the first time. She didn't know anything helpful then, so now she knows even—"

"Yes," Hallop said, cutting him off. "We're aware of the circumstances the first time. We're already co-operating with the RCMP on this. They obviously have an interest in what's happened now."

"And what, *exactly*, did happen now?" Logan asked.

Hallop gave him an annoyed glance, then nodded to Mitropoulos.

The younger man flipped back a few pages in his book and looked at Ali, as if she'd asked the question. "Mr. Weyden was killed by a semiautomatic pistol," he began, half reading, half watching Ali.

"We estimate the shooting occurred sometime between 3:00 and 5:00 a.m. A jogger found his body in High Park at approximately 8:00 a.m., but it had been taken to that location after he was killed. Our belief at this point, based on the wounds and other evidence, is that he was shot while in a car. He was likely the driver, which would explain why there were no other keys on his person. Our assumption is that they were left in the ignition," Mitropoulos concluded, glancing at Hallop.

"So, Mrs. Weyden," Hallop said, taking over again. "Were you aware your husband was actually alive? Had you seen him recently?"

"No," she whispered. "No, I hadn't seen him."

"Had you heard from him?"

"Wait a minute," Logan said before Ali could answer. "She just finished saying she didn't know he was alive. You've given her some shocking news, so I don't think—"

"Mr. Reed," Hallop snapped, "I'm afraid if you're going to interfere you'll have to leave."

"Detective Hallop," Ali said, her voice still a little shaky. "Logan isn't trying to interfere. But...I'm afraid I'm not feeling well right now. We just got back from visiting a friend who's *extremely* ill. She had surgery and...I'm sorry...I was very upset before you even got here...and hearing about Bob...I really can't cope with talking to you right now. Could we do it later? Maybe this evening? I could come to your office, or—"

"Mrs. Weyden, this is important."

"Yes, I understand that. You have a murder case on your hands. But I'm sure you don't suspect *me* of having killed my husband."

"No, of course not, but—"

"And nothing I can tell you will...what Logan said before is true. I didn't know anything that could help the RCMP last time, and there's nothing now that..." Ali dissolved into tears and buried her face in her hands.

Logan glared over her head at the detectives. "Can't you *see* the shape she's in? She was told eighteen months ago her husband was dead. And she thought that was true. What do you figure she can tell you now that can't wait a few hours?"

ALI SAT HUDDLED in her chair while Logan showed the detectives out. Even after she'd collapsed into tears, he'd had a hard time convincing them to leave, because they'd clearly suspected she was putting on a performance.

Of course, she *had* been trying to duck their questions, but it had hardly been a performance. All she'd done was stop trying *quite* so hard not to cry, and her tears had begun flowing as if they'd never stop. But now she had to pull herself together. She was so terrified she could scarcely think, yet she *had* to think.

Bob was dead. Really dead this time. The deal they'd made last night meant nothing any longer. He definitely wouldn't be sending Robbie back to her, which made it even more crucial that she find him— even though that was seeming more impossible than ever.

An image of Bob had formed in her mind and she closed her eyes. Her thoughts were so full of Robbie she hadn't really considered how she felt about Bob's murder. Surely nobody deserved to be shot to death by Nick Sinclair or his silent friend—whichever of them had pulled the trigger. She buried her face in her hands again, knowing she'd scraped the absolute bottom of her emotional reserve. But she had to hold on.

"Hey," Logan said.

When she looked, he was standing in front of her.

He rested his hands on her arms, drew her to her feet and pulled her tightly to him.

"We've got till seven tonight," he said quietly. "That's when Hallop and his buddy are coming back. And if we haven't found Robbie by then I think we're going to have to tell them everything. We can't play fast and loose with them forever."

Pressing her cheek against his chest, she couldn't help thinking that wasn't the only reason they'd have to tell the police everything. She might not write crime fiction, but she knew that when kidnappings went wrong, the kidnap victim usually ended up dead. And that meant if she and Logan didn't find Robbie soon, their likelihood of *ever* finding him alive would be frighteningly low.

If they didn't find him soon, telling the police the entire story and hoping for the best would be the only thing left to do. Regardless of Nick Sinclair's threats. She stood listening to the solid thudding of Logan's heart, telling herself over and over again that they *were* going to find Robbie soon.

Then the phone rang and she tensed.

"I'll get it," Logan said. He tentatively released Ali, half-afraid she wasn't up to standing on her own, let alone managing a phone conversation.

When he started for the kitchen, though, she was right on his heels.

The recorder was still connected to the phone, but he had to look twice to be sure it had come on. The afternoon sunlight filling the room made the red light's glow barely visible.

When he grabbed the receiver and said hello, a man demanded, "Who's that?"

It took half a second before he recognized the voice as Vinny Velarde's.

"It's Logan Reed. What can I do for you?"

"You can put Ali on."

He glanced at her, covering the mouthpiece with his hand and whispering, "Vinny."

"Oh, Lord," she whispered back. "We still don't know if he was really in cahoots with Bob or not. But if he was . . . Logan, if he was he might know where Robbie is."

"Do you want to do the talking?"

She pressed her fingers to her mouth and shook her head. "I'm so upset I can't think straight. Do you think you could get him to talk to you?"

"Sorry, Vinny," Logan said, "she can't come to the phone right now. She said to ask you what's up."

"What's up? Hell, you tell me what's up! I'm with a supplier all morning, and when I finally get to the office all I find is my machine full of messages I don't want to hear. First there's one from Deloras, telling me she's not coming in because she's sick. And there's one from my *wife.*"

Vinny paused, as if he expected Logan to know exactly what *that* message had been about. And guessing was hardly a challenge. Mimi had been so curious about why Vinny hadn't told her Bob was alive, she'd probably been on the phone to Custom Cargoes the very minute Logan and Ali had left the cottage.

"Mimi's going bananas, you know," Vinny went on when Logan didn't say anything. "Why would you go up there and tell her about Bob when I hadn't?"

"Why hadn't you?" Logan asked. That question had bothered him the entire drive back from Muskoka, and the answer might tell them, once and for all, if Vinny really knew anything about Robbie or not.

"Why?" he said. "Because she's an insane worrier, that's why. And when she worries she's constantly on my back. And as soon as it occurs to her that Bob's being alive means I owe the insurance company five million bucks, she's going to go nuts with worrying. So I figured I'd try to get things worked out somehow, before I told her."

Logan swore to himself. That had a strong ring of believability to it. And if Vinny hadn't been keeping Mimi in the dark because he'd been helping Bob, so much for his knowing where Robbie was.

"So?" Vinny snapped. "What was the deal with you and Ali going up there?"

"I take it you didn't call Mimi back and ask *her*?"

"Brilliant deduction, Sherlock. I'll let her calm down some, first. Besides, I got another message I wasn't too happy to hear. Some cop wants me to phone him. Urgent, he said. That was the whole message. But I figure it must be something to do with Bob. Or Sinclair. So does Ali know anything? Has something happened with her and Bob and the Robbie thing?"

"What was the cop's name?" Logan asked, certain he already knew.

"Lemme see what I wrote down... Hallop. Detective Frank Hallop. Why?"

"I figured it might be. We just had a visit from him."

"So it *is* something about Bob."

"Yeah, it is. He's dead, Vinny. Somebody shot him."

There was a long silence, and Logan would have bet the bank he knew what thoughts were going through Vinny's mind. He no longer had to worry about trying to get things worked out as far as his five million was concerned. They'd been worked out for him. His partner was dead, so that business insurance was legally his.

"Sinclair was the shooter?" he asked at last.

"That would be the obvious guess. The police don't seem to know it yet, though."

"What *do* they know?"

Logan hesitated. He and Ali were already skating on thin ice with the police, so maybe he should keep quiet. But, hell, Hallop and his partner were going to ask Vinny exactly what they'd asked Ali. The questions had hardly been state secrets.

"What did Ali tell them?" Vinny pressed.

"Not much. They were only here a few minutes. Somebody still has Robbie and we didn't want to sit around talking to the cops. We've got to find him."

"Right. Right... but just tell me what to expect so I don't get any surprises."

"I've already told you. They're going to tell you Bob was murdered. And I guess they'll ask you what they asked Ali. Whether she knew he was really alive, that kind of thing."

"So what did she say? She tell them about Robbie and everything?"

"No, she didn't tell them anything. We managed to put them off for the moment."

"Well, what the hell am I supposed to do, then? If I don't tell them she filled me in the other day, where does that leave me when they find out? Reed, I can do without having the cops on my back."

"Then I guess you'd better tell them the truth. The next time they come around, Ali's going to have to tell them everything, anyway."

"Oh . . . okay, then. So did they ask about anything else?"

"No, like I said, she just talked to them for a couple of minutes. The only other thing . . ."

"Yeah?"

Logan swore silently again. Why was he wasting time talking to Vinny? "A key," he said. "They asked if she knew about some safety deposit key they found on Bob. Told her the number on it and—"

"What was it?"

"I don't remember. Look, Vinny, I've got to go."

"Was it 3374?"

"Yeah . . . yeah, you know, I think that *was* it."

This time *Vinny* swore. But not silently. "That," he finally muttered, "is *our* safety deposit box number. *Mine,* I mean—Custom Cargoes'. And there's only one reason Bob would have been carrying it around after all this time—know what I mean?"

"No. What *do* you mean?"

"I mean my good old partner was intending to clean the box out on me before he disappeared again."

ONCE VINNY FINISHED ranting about his ex-partner and hung up, Ali wanted to hear both sides of the conversation. Logan rewound the tape and pressed the replay switch, but his conversation with Vinny wasn't the first one up. Before that began, the call telling Ali to go to the Velardes' cottage replayed. It began nagging at Logan while he listened to it, and stayed on his mind while the rest of the tape wound on.

"It wasn't Vinny after all, was it," Ali murmured when the conversation with him ended. "Twice, I was sure he was the one, but he wasn't."

"That woman who phoned is our clue," Logan said, hitting Rewind again. "Not the message, but her."

"You think so?"

Ali sounded as if she was completely out of hope, so he reached across and covered her hand with his.

She didn't even smile. He doubted she could have if she'd tried.

"I think she has to be," he said.

But what good was a clue when they didn't know what to make of it? What use had it been to borrow this recorder from his father when nothing they'd taped had helped them in the slightest?

The tape finished rewinding and he pressed Play again.

"Hello," the woman said once more. "Is this Ali Weyden?"

"Yes," said Ali's voice.

"I have a message for you, Mrs. Weyden. From your husband."

"Yes," Ali's voice said again.

Logan waited while faint background noise filled the following pause.

"The message," the woman finally began again, "is that—"

"Oh, jeez," he muttered. He stopped the tape mid-sentence and rewound it a little.

"What?" Ali said, gazing at him.

"Let's see just how good this baby is." He slid the recorder closer so he could read its dials more clearly.

"What?" Ali asked a second time.

"Look at all these controls. Remember, when I first brought it, I said it could do amazing things? Well, my father gave me a quick run-through, and this background enhance control is supposed to clarify that noise we're hearing. And I can really juice it up, so let's have a shot at it."

He turned the dial halfway, then tried the tape again.

A tiny shiver raced through Ali's entire body. "It's not just *noise* anymore. It sounds like a train."

"A *subway* train. That *has* to be what it is. No other train would pull in and out of a station that fast."

"And the other noise... Logan, it's a woman whispering. It's that same woman's voice, but I can't make out the words."

"I'll play it again. I didn't have it nearly as high as it can go."

Ali held her breath while he rewound the tape once more.

When he played it back this time, her hands flew to her ears. The volume was so loud the conversation level had risen from talking to screeching.

"From your husband," the woman screamed.

"Yes?" Ali's own voice screamed back.

The sound of the train was so clear they might have been in the subway station. And then they were able to make out what the woman was saying.

"Deloras," she whispered, "keep Robbie quiet, will you?"

"THAT'S ROYAL YORK ROAD we're coming to," Logan said, slowing for the red light ahead. "And Islington's the next major intersection after that, right?"

Ali nodded, still weak with relief that they'd finally learned who had her son—and that it wasn't Nick Sinclair. As much as she disliked Deloras Gayle, she was a far cry from a murdering gangster. And it *was* Deloras who had Robbie. This time, *all* the pieces fit.

Even though few women were listed in the phone book under their full names, there'd been a listing for a Deloras Gayle. And, given her address, the subway sounds made perfect sense. According to Logan's street guide, the number on Islington was at the corner of Bloor, which meant it was one of the big apartment towers that sat on top of the Islington subway station. It seemed most likely that the woman had been calling from a cell phone, inside Deloras's apartment.

Adding that to the unusual spelling of Deloras, the listing just had to be for *their* Deloras Gayle. Or Vinny's. Or maybe calling her Bob's Deloras would be the most accurate. Sometime during the past eighteen months, Bob must have gotten hold of his old girlfriend and enlisted her help. Or maybe she'd known all along that he was alive. Maybe she'd even helped plan his disappearance.

Whatever the details, while Deloras had been following her normal work routine this week, the picture of innocence, Robbie must have been right in her apartment, with the woman she and Bob had gotten to look after him. And now, in no time at all, they'd be reaching that apartment. So unless...

"What's the matter?" Logan said a second later, as if he could read her mind.

"I...I just can't help thinking that when they phoned it was nine o'clock this morning and now it's four in the afternoon. What if they're not still at the apartment?"

"They'll be there. Deloras had to have been waiting to connect with Bob—either expecting him to call or to arrive. So she won't have gone anywhere."

"But what if she was supposed to meet him someplace? What if that's how they'd arranged things?"

"Well...he certainly couldn't have shown up to meet her, could he," Logan said quietly. "And when he didn't, she'd have concluded something had gone wrong and come home—assuming he'd call her there."

"You're sure?"

"Positive."

Ali gazed out at the passing stores on Bloor, wondering if Logan was really as confident as he sounded. But *all* the pieces fit this time, she reminded herself. So he had every reason to be confident. And so did she.

"I should have realized it might have been Deloras, you know," she said at last. "*Especially* once we'd ruled out everyone else I could think of."

Logan shrugged. "Hindsight always makes things seem more obvious."

"Well...yes." But still, she should have at least *thought* of Deloras. After all, it had been Bob's fooling around with the woman that had been the final nail in the coffin of their marriage. And Deloras could have found out about the Christmas party simply by listening in on Vinny's line.

So why hadn't she and Logan put things together sooner, when now that they had it all seemed crystal clear? Bob had intended to clean out Custom Cargoes' safety deposit box this morning. Then he'd have taken off with Deloras today, instead of waiting until Friday and risking spending any longer in the same city as Nick Sinclair. But just by delaying his departure until today, Bob had waited too long.

"That's a good omen," Logan said, interrupting her thoughts. "There are spaces in the visitors' parking area."

He wheeled into one of them and she realized they'd arrived. They were surrounded by high rises, and in only a few more minutes they'd be standing outside Deloras Gayle's apartment. They wouldn't be standing in the hallway for long, though. They'd get inside if they had to kick the door in.

Despite an afternoon sun that was so bright Logan had been wearing sunglasses to drive, the temperature was dropping and a strong wind had come up. It was swirling nastily around the parked cars, so Ali and Logan hugged their scarves more tightly to their throats as they climbed out of the Jeep and hurried for the building.

When they reached it, there was no sign of a concierge beyond the glass interior doors. But there *was* a security lock system. Logan stuck his sunglasses in his pocket and started to check the names beside the buzzers. "She's in 2115," he finally announced.

"What?" Ali said anxiously. "The twenty-first floor? Logan, what about the subway noise. There's no way it could reach that high, is there?"

"Well . . . it must, because we heard it. So there has to be some weird sound drift or something. I think there's a principle of physics that would explain it . . . called the Doppler effect, I think."

There'd been too many "I thinks" in that explanation to give Ali any confidence. But she didn't know a damned thing about physics, so maybe he was right. Pushing the worry that he wasn't back behind all the other worries preying on her, she asked him how they were going to get inside.

"No problem. Go stand by the door until somebody unlocks it for us." He began pressing the buzzers, starting at the top of the first column and working his way down. After he'd tried half a dozen or so the lock buzzed and Ali pulled the door open.

Getting in had been so easy that she actually felt herself smiling. If the rest of the plan went as smoothly, she'd be with Robbie in only a few more minutes.

The thought made her heart sing. Then it began to pound as they rode the elevator up to the twenty-first floor.

Chapter Fifteen

The elevator doors opened on Deloras Gayle's floor and Logan took Ali's hand, saying, "It's almost over."

She tried to smile, but after all they'd been through, she wasn't going to count on anything being over until Robbie was safely back in her arms. They started off in the wrong direction, then had to retrace their steps. With each passing second, her heart was hammering harder.

"This is it," Logan whispered, stopping in front of 2115. He pulled his sunglasses from his pocket, put them on, then tugged up his scarf so it covered the bottom part of his face.

"You stay out of sight," he added, gesturing at the peephole.

Ali stood pressed against the wall after he'd knocked, straining to hear something from inside the apartment. But she couldn't hear a thing, let alone someone coming to the door. Apparently Logan couldn't, either, because he knocked a second time.

Panic began seeping through her when there was still no response. If Robbie wasn't in there . . .

"Keep an eye out," Logan said. "And if anyone comes into the hall, give me a quick poke."

She glanced either way down the empty corridor, then looked back at him. He'd produced some sort of little tool and was working away at the lock with it.

She watched, while what he was doing sank in. He was picking Deloras's lock. So *that's* how he'd gotten into Kent Schiraldi's apartment. Lord, when he'd told her he'd learned some useful tricks, doing research for his books, she'd never imagined *this* was one of them.

She checked both ways again, telling herself not to think about the fact that Robbie didn't seem to be here, where they'd counted on finding him, or about how the police would view Logan's little trick. And then she heard a quiet click and Logan was cautiously pushing the door open.

They stood listening to the silence for a moment, then slipped inside and closed the door.

Robbie definitely wasn't in the apartment. Ali was certain of that without taking another step, and it made her sense of panic almost impossible to control. She took a deep breath and tried with all her might not to let it overwhelm her.

"Come on," Logan said, reaching for her hand again. "Let's see if there's any sign he's been here."

There was nothing in the living room, kitchen or bathroom that hinted there'd ever been a child in Deloras's apartment. No toys, no childrens' games or clothes lying around, nothing. The bedroom was the last place they looked, and there was nothing apparent there, either.

Ali opened the sliding closet door, just in case...and found herself staring at a few odds and ends of clothing and a lot of empty hangers. "Oh, my God," she whispered. "Most of her clothes are gone."

Logan had a quick glance into the closet, then strode over to the dresser and yanked open a couple of drawers. "These are pretty empty, too," he muttered. "And there aren't any suitcases around, which means she must have already taken off. So let's get out of here."

They started back toward the front door, Ali numb to the point of feeling nothing. Her son wasn't here, where they'd been sure he'd be, and neither was Deloras. They'd gotten so near, but not near enough. And Ali was utterly terrified that they'd missed their only chance. She desperately wanted to ask Logan where they went from here, desperately needed him to have an answer, but the question refused to come out.

"Okay, what we do next," he said, going into his mind-reading routine again, "is try to find out where Deloras went. She must have taken Robbie with her, so we've got to figure out where they've gone."

The question *how?* wouldn't come out, either. So when Logan opened the door Ali simply followed along, down the hallway to the next apartment.

He knocked, but there was no answer. They tried the apartment across the hall, and when that produced no results they backtracked to the other side of Deloras's place and tried there.

Just as Ali was deciding every single resident in the building was at work, a woman called, "Coming."

"Bingo," Logan whispered.

They waited, Ali barely breathing, until the door opened on its chain.

"Yes?" a middle-aged woman said, peering out at them.

"Sorry to bother you," Logan said, "but do you know Deloras Gayle?"

"Why?" The woman glanced suspiciously from Logan to Ali, then back to Logan.

"Oh, it's nothing," he said. "I mean, there's no problem. It's just that she doesn't seem to be home. She told us to come around four, but..."

He paused while the woman checked her watch, then added, "We thought, if she figured there was a chance she'd be late, she might have asked one of her neighbors to watch for us or something."

"You friends of hers, then?"

"Yes," Ali said, almost surprised to discover her voice was working again. "We're *good* friends. From out of town."

"Well...she usually works till five. You're sure she said four?"

"Yes, she said she had the day off and she'd be here. You didn't see her go out or anything?"

"No, sorry." The woman shut the door.

Watching it close made Ali feel as if all hope was gone. They *had* missed their chance. Tears formed in her eyes, but before they began to spill over the door opened again.

"You could try asking her sister," the woman suggested. "They're always running back and forth, so Julie might be able to help you. Or you could wait in her place, maybe. She's between jobs, as she puts it, so she's usually home. She's down on the second floor. It's 207. No...yes...well, I *think* it's 207."

"Oh, great, thanks," Logan said. "I've never met Julie. But she's married, isn't she?"

The woman shrugged. "Not exactly. Divorced, I think. Or maybe just separated."

"Oh, well, I was only wondering about her last name—in case we have to double-check the apartment number."

"Mmm...it's Becker, I think. Yeah, I'm sure. Like that sleazy lawyer who usta be on "L.A. Law," you know?"

THEY WERE HALFWAY DOWN the second floor hall when Ali heard a faint rumbling noise.

For a moment she didn't realize what it was. Then she recognized it and her pulse began to race. The sounds from the subway trains definitely reached the second floor, and hearing them started her mind racing to conclusions...or was she *jumping* to conclusions again?

Logan squeezed her hand. "Sounds just like our tape, doesn't it? I guess it wasn't the Doppler effect after all."

"You really think we've got it right this time? You think *this* is where they were keeping him?" That seemed obvious to *her,* but so many times already...

"It makes perfect sense," Logan said. "A perfect hiding place. Even if you *had* suspected Deloras long ago you wouldn't have thought to check here. You didn't even know she had a sister, did you?"

Ali shook her head. "But even if Robbie *was* here... Logan, upstairs you said that wherever Deloras went, she must have taken Robbie with her. So even if he *was* here..."

"Maybe she *didn't* take him, though. When I said that, we didn't know about the sister. And if he isn't here...well, if he isn't, the sister will know where he is."

Despite his words, Logan didn't sound nearly as confident as he had earlier, and by the time they reached 207, Ali was practically shaking. She pressed her back against the wall beside the door, grateful for its support. From inside, the faint sounds of a television were audible. Somebody was in the apartment. But was Robbie there or not?

"Don't forget that neighbor wasn't sure about the number," Logan whispered, putting his sunglasses back on and adjusting his scarf over his face again. "If this isn't it, we'll have to go back down to the main floor and check the directory."

Logan knocked...and a moment later whispered, "Someone's coming."

Ali's breath caught in her throat. She was afraid even to hope, and yet...

"Yes?" a woman's voice said from inside.

"Courier," Logan said. "Delivery for Julie Becker."

"Open it," a second voice called, "it must be something from Bob. Finally, he deigns to let me know what the hell's going on. And only six hours late."

It was Deloras's voice! Ali was certain it was, and her heart began to pound.

She listened while someone slid the chain.

Then the door cracked open and Logan slammed it against the wall, shouldering his way in.

Ali followed him into the entrance hall, but stopped short as a shiver of terror raced through her. For the second time in one day a woman was pointing a gun at them. This time it was Deloras, standing not six feet away.

The woman who'd answered the door was pressing herself into the wall. In the living room, beyond Deloras, Ali could see two suitcases. But Robbie was nowhere in sight.

"Where's Robbie?" she whispered, almost too afraid to ask. "Deloras, where's my son?"

"What the hell's going on?" she demanded. "Did Bob tell you Robbie was here?"

"I told you not to trust him," the other woman muttered. "Didn't I say he'd pull something like this? Leave you high and dry?"

"Shut up, Julie," Deloras snapped, waving the gun for emphasis. "Why don't you go check on things in the bedroom?"

Julie scurried off and Ali followed with her eyes, her pulse racing crazily. Robbie had to be in that bedroom, only a few yards away, but—

"That's it, isn't it?" Deloras demanded. "Bob told you to come here and get Robbie, didn't he?"

Ali didn't know how to answer. What would happen if she told Deloras that Bob was dead? Would she get hysterical? With a gun in her hand?

"That's it, isn't it?" she asked again. "He took off without me, didn't he? After I even grabbed the damned kid for him. And did everything else, too, 'cuz Bob didn't want to see him."

"*You* took Robbie?" Ali whispered.

Deloras gave a derisive snort. "You didn't street-proof him too well, did you? I just said there was an extra present for him and he went with me."

"Look," Logan said, "let's cut to the chase, huh? Bob's left you in the lurch, so just let us have Robbie and—"

"Uh-uh," Deloras said, waving her gun again. "Maybe Bob *thinks* he pulled a fast one, but he's got a surprise coming. That two million bucks," she said to Ali. "I want you to phone your broker right now and change the plans. Tell him you don't want it transferred to Switzerland after all. Tell him you want it right in your hot little hands on Friday. *Then* we'll talk about you getting Robbie back.

"I said right now," she snapped when Ali didn't move. "There's a phone in the living room. You, too," she added to Logan.

Feeling as if she was in the midst of an endless nightmare, Ali began to move forward.

Logan started after her, praying for a chance at Deloras, but she was carefully keeping her distance.

Then, just as he and Ali reached the side hall, the bedroom door burst open and Robbie barreled out.

"Mommy!" he shouted, streaking toward her.

"Get back here," Julie screamed from behind him.

Deloras's gaze flickered to them.

Logan saw his chance and dove at her.

When he tackled her they both hit the floor and the gun went flying, but she scratched at his eyes and bit his hand so hard he let go of her. She scooted after the gun on her hands and knees and he barely managed to knock it away. Then she was on her feet again, and when he grabbed her wrists she tried to knee him in the groin. He wrestled her to the floor and finally managed to pin her.

"Damn you," she cursed beneath him, squirming with all her might. She wasn't strong enough to get away, though, and Logan quickly glanced over to where he'd last seen the gun, hoping Julie hadn't grabbed it.

She hadn't. It was still lying by a chair, and Julie was just standing in the hall, staring at them. Deciding she wouldn't be causing trouble, Logan looked at Ali. She was on her knees, holding Robbie in her arms, and seeing them together again made him feel so good he couldn't help smiling.

Ali gazed over Robbie's head at Logan, knowing that she'd never be able to thank him enough, knowing she'd never feel more relieved than she felt right now. She'd been so afraid she'd never hold Robbie again that he seemed like a miracle in her arms.

"Mommy, I'm so glad you finally came," he whispered.

She patted his back, wishing she could erase the past few days from his life. "I'm sorry it took so long," she murmured. "But are you all right?"

When he nodded she simply continued hugging him, loving his sturdy little-boyness. He felt so wonderful against her that she was never going to let him go.

LOGAN SAT at Ali's kitchen table, thinking what a long evening it had been. Hallop and Mitropoulos had taken forever getting their statements, but at least they'd been fast about catching up with Sinclair and Gonzalez. And at least they'd called to let Ali know the two were in custody.

As far as Robbie was concerned, he'd been examined by an entire medical team and pronounced physically unharmed.

Emotionally, too, he seemed great—remarkably unaffected by what had happened. But Ali had wanted advice from an expert she had faith in, so as soon as she'd tucked him into bed she'd called one of her professors, who was also the chief of psychology at the Toronto Children's Hospital.

Logan glanced over at her, standing by the counter with the phone in her hand, and decided that whatever the guy was telling her had to be good news. For the first time in days, she didn't look stressed out. What she looked was beautiful. So damned beautiful it hurt. How could he possibly go off to L.A. without her?

He couldn't. So he was going to have to convince her to go with him. They couldn't possibly be living thousands of miles apart when they were perfect together.

Hell, they were even good together as detectives. Bob's plan had turned out to be exactly what they'd figured. The wild-goose chase to Muskoka had been set up so Julie could take Robbie home, with no one there to see her, while Bob and Deloras were taking off for parts unknown.

But, of course, Bob's plan had run into a major hitch. And when he hadn't called Deloras in the morning to confirm that he'd cleaned out the safety deposit box and was ready to meet her, she'd kept Robbie where he was. Logan absently reached for the last chocolate chip cookie, then looked over at Ali once more.

"Well, thank you *so* much," she was saying. "Yes...yes, I'll have the best Christmas ever. You, too."

"So?" he asked as she hung up.

She leaned back against the counter and shrugged, but it was a happy, smiling shrug. "He said the after-effects of an experience like this can really vary, and he thought Robbie sounded like one of the lucky ones.

"He's offered to see him after Christmas, but he figures all I'll have to do is make sure his life gets back to normal—keep everything as stable as possible for the next few months."

"Sounds like sensible advice," Logan said. It sounded like a death knell, though, to the idea of Ali packing up and heading to L.A. with him. That sure wouldn't be keeping things stable. He pushed himself away from the table and paced unhappily across the room.

"You'll go pick up Cody in the morning?" she asked.

He nodded. "First thing. Then do you want me to bring him over here—help start getting things back to normal?"

"That would be great. I could make lunch...bake some more cookies," she added, glancing at the empty plate. "Oh, Logan, I'm just so happy to have him home."

"I know." He draped his arms around her waist and pulled her close. Her nearness was instantly arousing, but he tried to ignore the message his body was sending.

Last night, he'd been in her bed. But part of getting things back to normal meant separate beds again...separate houses. And soon, separate countries.

Doing his best not to think about that, he kissed her. She tasted sweeter than chocolate chips and smelled so enticing that his body's message was getting more urgent by the second. He wanted to spend the entire night making love to her. But that was impossible tonight, with Robbie just down the hall.

"I love you," he finally whispered.

"Oh, Logan, I love you, too."

But what the hell, he wondered, were they going to do about it?

ALI TOOK HER BATCH of cookies from the oven, absently listening to the little-boy noises drifting down from Robbie's bedroom. For all her fears that he might have been traumatized by the kidnapping, so far there'd been no sign of any negative effects. He'd slept soundly through the night, and now he and Cody were right back into the swing of things.

They'd even invented a new game that involved impersonating Santa's reindeer—all of them at once, from the sounds of it. She smiled to herself. Then she glanced over to where Logan was standing at the window and her smile faded.

She was so very happy, yet just looking at him made her begin thinking thoughts that marred her happiness. She had her son back, but in only a few weeks she was going to lose Logan.

Already, he seemed distant. He hadn't kissed her good morning when he'd arrived, and even though she'd told herself it was because the boys had been right there, she knew something was bothering him.

Instead of sitting down and making himself at home, he'd been wandering uneasily around the kitchen, as if he had something to say but wasn't sure how to put it. And she had a horrible suspicion she knew what it was.

He, too, had to be thinking about how soon he'd be leaving. And even though he'd told her they'd some-how work things out...

But he'd said that in the warmth of her bed. And cold reality had a way of making that sort of promise seem foolish.

If she lost him, though...she loved him so much, how could she bear to lose him?

"Ali?" he said quietly, drawing her attention back to the moment.

Waiting for him to go on, she couldn't help think-ing he was the absolute ideal man for her. But he was going to slip through her fingers like quicksilver, and there wasn't a thing she could do to prevent it.

"There's something I have to tell you," he said.

She nodded, afraid her voice would betray her if she spoke, knowing he was going to tell her that the promise he'd made in the heat of passion—

"I'm not going to L.A."

She just stared at him, not certain she'd heard him right.

"I called my agent before Cody and I came over—explained that circumstances had changed and I just couldn't leave Toronto right now."

"But...but you said it's the chance of a life-time...your chance to be rich and famous."

He shrugged. "There might be some way of work-ing things out. Phones, faxes, the whole superinformation highway. And if we *can't* do things long-distance...well, there are more important things than being rich and famous...don't you think?''

"Oh, Logan," she whispered.

He took a step toward her and she flung herself into his arms, so happy she was crying.

"Hey!" a thin little voice said behind them. "What are you two doing? Look at them, Cody. They're hugging. Yuuuuckkk!"

"Yuuuuckkk!" Cody repeated. "Hey, Dad, guess what?"

"What?" Logan released Ali, but kept one arm firmly around her waist.

"Me an' Robbie decided we're gonna be blood brothers. So we gotta cut our thumbs and moosh the blood together, okay? 'Cuz that's the way you gotta do it."

"Oh?" Logan smiled at Ali. "I think there might be a less painful way for them to be brothers, don't you? If it wouldn't be making things unstable."

"I don't think it would be making things unstable at all," she murmured.

Logan's smile grew. Then he put both arms around her again and kissed her.

"Yuuuuckkk!" two little voices chorused.

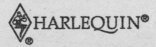

Fifty red-blooded, white-hot, true-blue hunks
from every State in the Union!

Look for MEN MADE IN AMERICA! Written by some
of our most popular authors, these stories feature fifty
of the strongest, sexiest men, each from a different state
in the union!

Two titles available every month at your favorite
retail outlet.

In December, look for:

NATURAL ATTRACTION by Marisa Carroll
(New Hampshire)
MOMENTS HARSH, MOMENTS GENTLE by Joan Hohl
(New Jersey)

In January 1995, look for:

WITHIN REACH by Marilyn Pappano (New Mexico)
IN GOOD FAITH by Judith McWilliams (New York)

You won't be able to resist MEN MADE IN AMERICA!

This holiday, join four hunky heroes under
the mistletoe for

Christmas
Kisses

Cuddle under a fluffy quilt, with a cup of hot chocolate and these
romances sure to warm you up:

#561 HE'S A REBEL (also a Studs title)
Linda Randall Wisdom

#562 THE BABY AND THE BODYGUARD
Jule McBride

#563 THE GIFT-WRAPPED GROOM
M.J. Rodgers

#564 A TIMELESS CHRISTMAS
Pat Chandler

Celebrate the season with all four holiday books sealed with a
Christmas kiss—coming to you in December, only from
Harlequin American Romance!

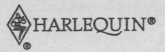 **HARLEQUIN®**

The proprietors of Weddings, Inc. hope you
have enjoyed visiting Eternity, Massachusetts.
And if you missed any of the exciting Weddings,
Inc. titles, here is your opportunity to complete
your collection:

Harlequin Superromance	#598	*Wedding Invitation* by Marisa Carroll	$3.50 U.S. ☐ $3.99 CAN. ☐	
Harlequin Romance	#3319	*Expectations* by Shannon Waverly	$2.99 U.S. ☐ $3.50 CAN. ☐	
Harlequin Temptation	#502	*Wedding Song* by Vicki Lewis Thompson	$2.99 U.S. ☐ $3.50 CAN. ☐	
Harlequin American Romance	#549	*The Wedding Gamble* by Muriel Jensen	$3.50 U.S. ☐ $3.99 CAN. ☐	
Harlequin Presents	#1692	*The Vengeful Groom* by Sara Wood	$2.99 U.S. ☐ $3.50 CAN. ☐	
Harlequin Intrigue	#298	*Edge of Eternity* by Jasmine Cresswell	$2.99 U.S. ☐ $3.50 CAN. ☐	
Harlequin Historical	#248	*Vows* by Margaret Moore	$3.99 U.S. ☐ $4.50 CAN. ☐	

HARLEQUIN BOOKS...
NOT THE SAME OLD STORY

TOTAL AMOUNT	$
POSTAGE & HANDLING	$
($1.00 for one book, 50¢ for each additional)	
APPLICABLE TAXES*	$ _____
<u>**TOTAL PAYABLE**</u>	$ _____
(check or money order—please do not send cash)	

To order, complete this form and send it, along with a check or money order for the
total above, payable to Harlequin Books, to: **In the U.S.:** 3010 Walden Avenue,
P.O. Box 9047, Buffalo, NY 14269-9047; **In Canada:** P.O. Box 613, Fort Erie, Ontario,
L2A 5X3.

Name: _____

Address: _____ City: _____

State/Prov.: _____ Zip/Postal Code: _____

*New York residents remit applicable sales taxes.
Canadian residents remit applicable GST and provincial taxes.

WED-F

HARLEQUIN®

I N T R I G U E®

Into a world where danger lurks around
every corner, and there's a fine line between trust
and betrayal, comes a tall, dark and handsome man.

Intuition draws you to him...but instinct keeps you
away. Is he really one of those

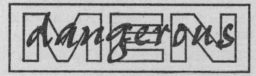

Don't miss even one of the twelve sexy but secretive
men, coming to you one per month, starting in
January 1995.

**Take a walk on the wild side...with our
"DANGEROUS MEN"!**

DM-G

Where do you find hot Texas nights, smooth Texas charm and dangerously sexy cowboys?

Crystal Creek reverberates with the exciting rhythm of Texas. Each story features the rugged individuals who live and love in the Lone Star state.

"...Crystal Creek wonderfully evokes the hot days and steamy nights of a small Texas community...impossible to put down until the last page is turned."
—*Romantic Times*

"With each book the characters in Crystal Creek become more endearingly familiar. This series is far from formula and a welcome addition to the category genre."
—*Affaire de Coeur*

"Altogether, it couldn't be better." —*Rendezvous*

Don't miss the next book in this exciting series. Look for
THE HEART WON'T LIE by MARGOT DALTON

Available in January wherever Harlequin books are sold.

CC-23